GW01085758

ABOUT ....

Frank Ahern is a graduate of Trinity College, Dublin. He has spent much of his life working in the home counties and now lives in Dorset, enjoying its rich natural world.

His first novel, *A Parcel of Fortunes*, was published in 2017.

He is currently working on *Russian Doll,* a sequel to *Ghost-lines,* in which Nick Barry is reunited with George Nelson.

GHOST-LINES

Frank Ahern

Matador
9 Priory Business Park,
Wistow Road, Kibworth Beauchamp,
Leicestershire. LE8 0RX
Tel: 0116 279 2299
Email: books@troubador.co.uk
Web: www.troubador.co.uk/matador
Twitter: @matadorbooks

ISBN 978 1838595 463

British Library Cataloguing in Publication Data.
A catalogue record for this book is available from the British Library.

Printed and bound in Great Britain by 4edge Limited
Typeset in 12pt Jenson Pro by Troubador Publishing Ltd, Leicester, UK

Matador is an imprint of Troubador Publishing Ltd

For Sue, Poppy and Dom

Contents

PART I

GHOSTING

1

I was busy one Friday afternoon ghosting a well-known footballer's column for a Sunday newspaper when the phone rang. It was Theresa d'Abruzzi. The lovely Theresa. The persuasive Theresa who, for all too short a time, managed to enchant me out of the routine dullness of my working life into a heady, error-strewn project. A helter-skelter venture that would jeopardise the professional reputation I had built up over many years.

She had found details of my freelancing career on the internet and wanted to explore my possible suitability for what she called 'an exciting and potentially huge project'. She sounded young and, in so far as one can tell over the phone – which isn't very far – quite sexy.

I have worked with all kinds of people whose names you will know. Pop stars, footballers, actors, politicians, many big celebrities. Celebs. Slebs. Some I have befriended, albeit at a superficial and normally fairly temporary level. And one, a footballer who shall remain nameless (for the time being only, perhaps), took friendship just a little bit too far, destroying my marriage by bedding my then wife.

I have spent many hours of my life toiling to transmute the dull and often leaden utterances of inarticulate slebs into the deathless prose of a best-selling autobiography or the sparkling journalese of a newspaper column; or at least into a language that captures and shares with a wider audience something of their celebrity lives. If you have read these people, then I must tell you that the words you may perhaps have assumed were theirs were sometimes actually mine. Mine was the ventriloquist's voice of the dummy or – to elevate the metaphor a little – the promethean fire that animated their breathy stories.

But this tale is not about any of these golden people, whose glitter will no doubt quickly tarnish. It is about an extraordinary man whose name will be unfamiliar to most of you. A man whose remarkable life I was asked to transcribe into the most incredible story. He is dead now. And of course dead men tell no lies. So it is left to me to breathe life once more into a fabulous tale. The ghost to reinvigorate the lifeless cadaver.

Whilst I have almost always been an outsider to the action I have described in the books I have ghosted – I am normally a mere scribe being bidden to look upon the lives of others without being drawn too closely in – very occasionally I have been a minor participant, taken up onto the stage to play a small role; a humble spear-carrier, if you will. In the story I am about to tell you, I was both within and without, watching from the wings, making the occasional entrance on cue.

When Theresa d'Abruzzi rang me that Friday afternoon, it was to tell me about her father, Carlo, the firecracker who kindled the sixties into a new way of being; and to sound me out about writing a book about him. She wanted us to meet at her flat in Hammersmith. However, I have always believed that the first face-to-face contact with a potential client should be on neutral ground. So we agreed on a café at Kew, halfway between her home and mine in Kingston.

I arrived early and waited patiently, scouring the door for likely entrants. I imagined, from the voice I had heard on the phone, that Theresa would be a young woman, in her twenties perhaps. And sexy, too, the voice had suggested. Two young women earned a second glance from me as they came in, but went to the counter to order straight away, not looking round for anyone – me; so I discounted them. And then in came Theresa, briskly glancing around the room until our eyes met and we smiled simultaneously.

'Nick Barry?' she asked, more as a statement than a question, as I stood and held out my hand.

'Hello, Theresa. What can I get you?'

As I waited at the counter to pay for coffees and the muffin she had asked for, I reflected on the accuracy of the intimation her alluring telephone voice had given me. Slightly built, she moved with an energy that seemed to contain a powerful latency within it, like a thoroughbred racehorse, perhaps. And her face was indeed beautiful, the sharp outline softened by the flawless youthful bloom of her skin, her blue eyes suggesting the wide-eyed openness of a child. I am of an age where a young and beautiful woman can be intimidating to the older man, but there was nothing threatening about Theresa at all. She would later tell me that she was the deputy practice manager for a large West London GP surgery, and certainly there was something matter-of-fact and business-like about her from the start.

5

But what most came across most strongly was her girlish enthusiasm and her evident delight in talking about her father.

She asked me if I knew the name Carlo d'Abruzzi and, when I said I didn't, she said, 'Charlie Adams? He sometimes used to go by that name.' I shook my head. 'It doesn't surprise me you haven't heard of him. So few people have these days. But he was a hugely important figure in the 1960s, seminal you might say. And it is because I want his name to get the recognition it deserves that I want a book written about him.'

Various questions were immediately springing to mind. What sort of book? Was the father still alive to be interviewed? What papers had been kept? Was there any kind of family archive of his 1960s activities? Were there other people I could interview, talk to? Was she expecting me to research, write and find a publisher for the book? What was she expecting to pay me for my time?

But I thought it best to take things slowly. 'Tell me why your father is interesting,' I said. 'Why he is worth writing a book about?'

And she was off. Listening to the fervour in that wonderful voice, catching a sense of her complete faith, her love, her uncompromising admiration of her father, completely hooked me and made me determined to take on the commission, assuming she was happy that I was the right person. She told me that her father was the man who first drew Brian Epstein's attention to the Beatles, though other people continued to claim the credit. She said he had seen Epstein a few months before his tragic death and had been very upset at the state he had found him in. She talked about a great poetry event he had organised at the Albert Hall in 1965, and about how it was he who had first suggested to Mary Quant that she introduce the famous monochrome geometrical shapes to her fashions.

'He sounds really interesting,' I said. 'Is he still alive?'

She nodded vigorously, but a shadow quickly passed over her face. 'He is, but he is becoming very forgetful. He's in the early stages of dementia…That's why I want this book written now.'

'You want it written by someone else? Has he never thought of writing it himself?'

She shook her head. 'No, and I think that is beyond him now. And in any case, he has never been keen. To be honest, he is not keen on a book being written about him at all.'

'He was never tempted to write an autobiography?'

'No. He didn't seem interested. I did suggest it. And, to encourage him, I spent a summer holidays, when I was in the sixth form, interviewing him on tape.' She smiled a lovely smile. 'So many wonderful anecdotes! He is… was… is… a natural storyteller… But the mind is going now, so I need someone to tell his story for him.'

'And why do you think I am the person to do it?' I asked.

'Just a hunch,' she said. 'I did lots of research on the internet into freelance writers, ghostwriters. I liked the way you wrote about yourself on your webpage and I like the blog you write… And I thought you had a nice face!' I was slightly taken aback by this comment. Was she flirting with me? Of course daddy's girls, if that's what she was, are well practised in manipulating older men to their wills. It's a charm they learn at a very early age.

'It seems a little tenuous!' I said with a chuckle.

'But I've also read some of your books. Even when you're writing about an individual, you seem to capture the background, the setting so well… But there are another couple of people I'm going to see before I make my final decision.'

I was disappointed to hear this. Although we had not discussed money or practicalities, still less had I discussed it with my agent, I wanted the project. 'And tell me,' I said, 'do you want the book written by me as me, or ghosted by me in your father's voice? Or your voice, even?'

She was unsure but inclined to go for a first-person narrative, the telling of the story in a style that captured her father's true voice. She was surprised that I couldn't guarantee publication. I explained that if my literary agent were to approach a publisher with a book I had ghosted for David Beckham or Mick Jagger, it would be snapped up with a huge advance just like that, but that a book about an unknown figure – relatively unknown, I corrected myself when I saw her expression – would be harder to place.

When we parted, she gave me warm peck on the cheek and said she would be in touch within the fortnight. Six days later she rang to say that she would like me for the project if we could work out a satisfactory arrangement, and she invited me for lunch in her Hammersmith flat the following week.

I have to admit that I spent much of the time looking forward to seeing Theresa again, to getting to know her better. All my successful projects have depended upon a good relationship with the client. If I want to inhabit my subject, to assume an accurate and compelling voice, I have to live inside them; I have got to befriend them so that I can get to know them as fully as possible. Of course Theresa was not, strictly speaking (or even loosely speaking), the subject of the book, but I sensed that the relationship with her was going to be key to the success of the project and I was excited at the prospect of working with her.

*

We were sitting out in Theresa's tiny garden. She had led me straight through her small basement flat just off Hammersmith Grove, up three steps to the bricked patio. A table had been laid and, although it was still early May, a large sun shade raised.

'I thought we'd eat out. I've prepared a coronation chicken and pavlova so I didn't have to do any cooking while you were here. But let's start with a drink.' There was the same business-like manner I had noted when I first met her, but also a jolliness and warmth that made me feel at ease.

Over a glass of dry Riesling I explained to her what had to be done first: the chapter-by-chapter outline that my agent would need to show to prospective publishers. 'I'll want to know at the outset what materials are available to me. How much I can interview your father—'

'Well, of course we have the interviews I did a few years back. I've still got the cassettes!' She giggled. 'How exciting!'

'And rather than a full biography, the publisher will probably want a narrowish focus, the sixties, for—'

'But his whole life is interesting!' Once again flooding excitement spilt into her voice. 'His great-grandfather was King Victor Emmanuel II of Italy... And his grandmother was Maria Bonaparte, whose great-uncle was Napoleon... I think I've got that right. Papa's told me enough times! His lineage is surely an important part of his story, no?'

'We'll see, we'll see.' I loved Theresa's enthusiasm but was beginning to worry that it might get in the way of the proper research I'd need to do.

When I asked her what her father did in the 70s and 80s and 90s, she told me that he'd become a lecturer in Contemporary Cultural Studies. He moved from London to the south coast. What had started as Institute of Higher Education had been elevated to a university by the time he retired, being briefly a polytechnic in the interim. 'Of course he was ideally equipped to teach young people about contemporary culture and about the enormous changes in the post-war years,' she told me.

I established that her father still lived near the south coast, in the small market town of Wimborne Minster, and I asked her to arrange a meeting for us.

We talked about ourselves for the rest of the lunch. She had wanted to be a doctor, she told me, but had ignored her school's advice that she probably wouldn't get the A level grades required. When, as predicted, she was given no offers for medical school, she had decided to do a City and Guilds Diploma in Primary Care and Health Management. 'Papa was so disappointed I didn't try for uni, but I'm very happy doing what I do. It's very satisfying work, though always a battle to keep within budget targets... And what about you? You've been a freelance writer most of your life, haven't you, Nick? According to the blurb on your website.' She giggled again. More a throaty gurgle. A slight draught of air lifted her hair from the side of her pale neck and rippled through her blue floral print dress.

'Yes. But a very varied career... a career with troughs and peaks, for sure!'

'Who's the most interesting person you've ever written about?'

I told her that all the people I'd written about were interesting, or I wouldn't have written about them.

'Who was the most difficult person? Time for teacher to tell tales!'

Was that how she saw me? I wondered She must have been very aware of the age difference. Unsurprising, of course.

I told her about a socialite I used to write for, penning her weekly column for a Sunday paper. 'She was the greatest of fun and very well connected and would sometimes tell me these amazing stories that I couldn't let anywhere near the paper. She would laugh and call me a custardy coward!'

'Why was that difficult?'

'That wasn't what was difficult. She'd had a drug problem but had got clean. But then she started drinking, gradually more and more, and finally went back to drugs as well. It was heart-breaking to watch her decline, to see her slowly killing herself... But she had an attractive, generous nature, and that never entirely disappeared. I used to enjoy our weekly meetings or phone calls. I was very, very sad when she died.'

'But why on earth didn't you try to stop her?'

'That wasn't down to me. In my work I have to be detached – the passive observer, the objective recorder. I can't interfere. It would change my role, ruin the neutral stance I have to take.'

Theresa wanted to know if I was married. I told her I was divorced, without going into any detail. She, I imagined, had queues of young men – and older men too, no doubt – lining up for her favours, but I didn't ask her to confirm or deny my suspicions.

She said she would find some possible weekends when we could go down to Dorset to see her father. And then it was time for me to go.

2

Theresa has a twin brother, Luca. Brother and sister were a late windfall for Carlo and his wife, Brenda, whom he had married in 1978. They had tried for over ten years to have a child and it was only once they had given up any real hope that they were blessed with the gift of not one but two. These details of her family I learnt from Theresa as we drove down to Dorset. I learnt too that Brenda, fifteen years younger than Carlo, had died of a late-diagnosed cancer when the twins were only nine. That Carlo had not remarried. That he had been a wonderful single parent. And that Theresa could see the day coming, as the dementia took hold, when she would have to mother her beloved father.

Not all the talk was gloomy and, as the M27 narrowed to become the A31, with cattle and ponies grazing the New Forest heathland either side of the road, Theresa's face broke into a sweet smile. 'This is always where I begin to feel that I am nearly home! I just love this part of the country.'

'It's impressive, isn't it? I haven't been down this way for years and years.'

Earlier in the drive, Theresa had asked me to be very patient with her father. 'Papa is slow these days. And, as I told you before, he doesn't really feel he is worthy of a book being written about him. So he might be a bit awkward.'

'Don't worry, Theresa. Patience is a prerequisite of my job. Over the years I've had to get to know all kinds of people. Have had to give them confidence in me so that I can get a real sense of who they are. With some the process is quick and easy – they want to be known, they want you to know every nook and cranny of their lives and they will talk and talk and then talk some more. The problem, often, is sifting what is useful and useable! With others there is a block, a kind of veil, a reticence, perhaps, which makes the whole process much more difficult. Sometimes it can be a little like an over-long chess match.'

'It sounds exciting... You must have developed all kinds of techniques.'

'That makes it sound rather more sinister than it really is. I'm just trying to get people to trust me, to trust me with their stories and to trust in my ability to shape them into interesting narratives... Unless, of course, I'm writing someone's newspaper column, in which case I'm trying to find the voice and the point of view appropriate to the person.'

*

The house was an attractive Edwardian semi, approached by car along a narrow lane that led to the bottom of the garden. What once had probably been well tended, with curving herbaceous borders, strategically placed shrubs and a neat lawn, was now showing signs of neglect. The grass had become tussocky and weed-filled and, overturned on one of the flowerbeds, lay a disintegrating wheelbarrow. A broken bird feeder contained a damp, blackened, congealed mess of food long ignored by any passing bird. Leaning against a decrepit shed was a lady's bicycle, with a sagging, rusty chain. I presumed it was Theresa's, carelessly abandoned when she moved to London.

As we got out of the car Carlo appeared at the kitchen door, waving warmly. He looked sprightly and youthful and handsome for a man of nearly eighty. His white hair was of the same cut and length as in a picture of the younger man I had seen in Theresa's flat. His face had a shiny, soapy texture, coloured in places by small webs of thread-veins, and a trickle of tear from a moist eye glistened on the side of his nose. Father and daughter embraced fiercely and then Theresa introduced me.

The gaze he gave me as I shook his hand was long and steady. It was not the slightly absent stare of someone with dementia, albeit in the early stages. It was the look of a protective father sizing me up. It was the look of a man issuing a challenge, a warning: I am in charge here; know your place. Once the look had communicated its message, the face loosened into a smile and some warmth crept into the eyes.

Over lunch Carlo talked mainly to Theresa, who found every opportunity she could to try to bring me into the conversation. But Carlo was more interested in his daughter. How her work was going, when she last saw her brother, when she'd move out of London and return to Dorset. The last question was awkward. She knew she would need to move soon, realised that perhaps she should be looking at GP practices in the area for an opening. I knew that she didn't really feel ready for this yet, but she didn't tell her father this.

He asked me if I was married and when I said not any more he asked, 'Dead?'

'No. No, we divorced a few years ago.'

'Anyone in tow?'

'No one special.'

He said life as a singleton was lonely. With no one to chat to, you forgot how to talk.

I hoped this was not entirely true. I was relying on his talk. I needed it so that I could write the book that Theresa wanted me to write. On the journey down, I had suggested to her that it would best if I had some time alone with her father; that perhaps the two of us could go for a walk together after lunch.

So, obligingly, once the plates had been cleared away, Theresa suggested breezily that we two men walk by the river. Carlo's face looked as though as it was about to break into a rebellious glower, the eyes sparkling dissent, but, with a little twitch in the corner of the mouth, quickly became the image of duteous resignation. The apparent sprightliness I had noticed when he had first greeted us at the kitchen door had gone. He put on his coat with difficulty, Theresa guiding his stiff arms awkwardly into the sleeves. And then we walked slowly away from the house, Carlo moving with short, flat-footed steps, which gradually loosened into something more fluent.

I had already decided that the main thrust of the book would be Carlo's contribution to the cultural revolution of post-war Britain. But I wanted to know more about the sort of man I was dealing with before getting to the fine detail of his life in the 1960s. I asked him what had brought him to the sleepy backwater of Dorset, after the febrile excitements of swinging London.

'I thought the movement had gone as far as it could.' I wasn't sure exactly what movement he was referring to, but I let him continue. 'I wanted a change. I saw a new post advertised in an Institute of Higher Education down here, so I applied for it.'

'Cultural Studies.'

'Yes, and I had the freedom pretty much to devise my own course.'

There was a splash as a swan came gliding down onto the river, inclining its webbed feet to brake against the water, followed almost immediately by a second.

'That must have been interesting.'

He told me that people of his generation were impatient. 'Their parents had fought a long and destructive war which was still being paid for a decade later by a sluggish economy weighted down in austerity. When things loosened a little, when young people began to have a bit of money of their own, they decided to spend it on what they wanted. And what they wanted was music of their own, fashion of their own, art of their own, writing of their own, morality of their own. They stopped listening to their parents. What did they know, the parents? About anything except war?' There was something sing-song in the voice, something incantatory, as though this was a remembered speech.

And what about his own parents, I asked him.

'Oh, that's not interesting. History no one is interested in. I suppose Theresa told you about my royal ancestry. It seems important to her. But really it isn't.' The voice was matter-of-fact, but the eyes took on a curious darting quality, as though he was suspicious of my response.

'Well, I think it is interesting. The scattering of European royals after two cataclysmic wars. I don't suppose I'll write at length about it, but I would like to hear a little about your ancestry.'

He cleared his throat in an irritated way and then glared at me. 'Oh, if you must.' And then, strangely, he assumed the same incantatory tone he had been using a little earlier, giving that same impression of rehearsed speech. 'My mother, Maria, a beautiful woman by all accounts, married my father Prince Umberto when she was very young. He was a fine man who fought bravely in the First World War and was decorated. He fought with the Royal Italian Army, for the Allied side, of course. Umberto was the son of Maria Letizia Bonaparte, and the grandson of Victor Emmanuel II, the first king of a united Italy. So yes, I am of royal descent but actually am a bit of a mongrel. The royal houses of Europe are very intermingled... And I suppose you want to know how I ended up in England.' I nodded. 'I was born in Trieste, a truly cosmopolitan city in the inter-war years. But as the war approached, the Germans exercised increasing influence in Northern Italy, and Trieste became a very fractured place.'

A rowing VIII of schoolboys came around a bend in the narrow river. On the towpath on the far bank was a man with a loudhailer shouting obscenities at the crew. 'Gosh,' I said, 'whoever would have thought that you could row on this narrow, bendy river?'

Carlo looked startled by my interruption and a little irritated. 'Where was I...? Where was I...? I was born in Trieste, a truly cosmopolitan city in the inter-war years. But as the war approached, the Germans exercised increasing influence in Northern Italy, and Trieste became a very fractured place. My mother had died when I was young and in 1940 my father was killed in a plane crash. I was six at the time. My nanny had friends in England, and thought it best that we escape Europe altogether and live with them. They kindly took me in and brought me up. Devon, we lived. Very fine people.' Carlo had a rich, sonorous baritone voice which showed no sign of his age. The accent carried no trace of his Italian heritage, nor of his West Country upbringing. If the standard, educated accent had any underlay at all, it was the merest tinge of London, heard in his slight curving of the '-ou-' dipthong.

We walked on in silence for a while. Apart from the foul-mouthed rowing coach and the odd squawk of a duck, it was a peaceful afternoon. I enjoyed watching the slow movement of the water, my reverie broken only momentarily by a flashing of turquoise and orange as a kingfisher flitted by, following the ribbon of river.

After Carlo suggested we turn back he asked me about my writing. I explained to him that I had spent all my career writing the words of others.

'Not really proper writing, is it?' The tone was dismissive, with just a hint of aggression to it.

But I didn't want to argue, so I let the remark go. 'No, I suppose it isn't, really.' And we walked on in silence.

*

When we arrived back at Carlo's house he said he was going upstairs for a short rest. Theresa was busy in the kitchen preparing a casserole for the evening. 'How did you get on?' she asked me.

'A start!' I said. 'But not very far, I'm afraid to say.'

'Oh… Was there a problem?'

'Not really a problem. He just seems very defensive. Suspicious of what I might be up to.'

She left her preparations for a moment and looked at me solemnly. 'You know, I'm sure it's the dementia… the onset of dementia that makes him grumpy sometimes and makes him seem a little defensive. He finds it harder to cope with new things, new people, perhaps with you. It'll take time, I'm sure.'

'Well, yes, I'm sure you're probably right… What I really need to know at this stage is what materials there are here for me to draw on.'

'You must ask him to take you into his study and show you what's available.'

Over the meal I once again felt like an eavesdropper on father and daughter, who seemed to be repeating a familiar routine of mutual admiration.

'You know, I am so proud of you, Theresa. The work you do for the NHS. People think it's all about doctors and nurses, but the administrators are just as important. They take the pressure off the doctors. They find ways of making the money go round, of ensuring the GPs get the proper training and latest medicines.'

She patted her father's hand. 'Oh, Papa, you make it sound more important than it is. Anyway, Nick doesn't want to hear about me, he wants to hear about you. You are much more interesting.'

'Did I tell you I was descended from kings?' And before I could tell him that, yes, he had, he was away. 'My mother,

Maria, a beautiful woman by all accounts, married my father Umberto when she was very young. He was a fine man who fought bravely in the First World War and was decorated. He fought with the Royal Italian Army, for the Allied side, of course.' I looked, possibly in mild alarm, at Theresa, who immediately understood what was going on but gave a little nod of the head and slight gesture with her hands to indicate that I should let him continue. So I heard once more about the pedigree, the birth in Trieste and the flight to England.

'That's fascinating, Carlo,' I said, drawing a relieved smile from Theresa. 'And I would love to know about your later life, about your lecturing, perhaps.'

'Of course,' he said.

'Perhaps tomorrow morning we could go to your study and have a look at some of the papers and things you have.'

I got the glare again. Penetrating. The eyes not darting, but unmoving, sharply pointed and unsoftened by the watery film that covered them. The Roman nose, curving elegantly from a high bridge, seemed to quiver. And the glare then seemed to retreat into itself, becoming the look, perhaps, of someone feeling threatened.

'We can discuss that tomorrow,' Theresa said, sensing the moment of tension.

Carlo's mood brightened after the meal when Theresa suggested that we play a game of Scrabble. 'Excellent idea, darling!'

Once the table had been cleared, he laid out a battered board and tipped the faded wooden squares beside it, turning them all over so that the letters were hidden, and then shuffling the tiles about. As he was doing this he explained what he called the House Rules. Thirty points, rather than the official fifty, for using all seven letters in one go; successful challenges – verified by the dictionary – resulting in the points value of the challenged word being taken from the transgressor, unsuccessful challenges resulting in the points value being deducted from the challenger. 'And players should not take too long taking their go,' he added.

'Always very subjective!' Theresa said playfully. 'And dependent upon how long Papa feels he needs for his go!'

'Cheeky monkey! I'll have you know I'm always very quick,' he replied with a chortle.

It fell to me to open the game, having drawn a 'B' at the start. Bereft of a good set of letters and lacking in imagination, I came up with 'BARES', which got me twenty points.

'You could have had BEARS,' said Theresa. 'Grrr!'

'I could have, but I wanted BARES. As in "Carlo bares all".'

This drew a sharp scowl from Carlo and I immediately regretted my teasing comment. He was in his best form of the day and it was foolish to jeopardise his genial mood.

'Or,' I said, 'SABRE,' duly rearranging the letters and miming the brandishing of a sword.

Theresa was the next to go and spent an inordinate amount of time shuffling her letters. With each rearrangement, her smile broadened. And then, with a triumphant beam, she laid out her word smartly, three letters above the 'E' of my word, four below: VENETIAN. 'Ta da! All seven letters! Bonus! Bonus!'

'Erm, you can't have proper nouns, I'm afraid, Theresa darling. Sorry!'

'Is it a proper noun, Papa?'

'Venetian. Venice. Place.'

I probably would have been better staying out of this minor family disagreement, but I decided to chip in. 'But it can be an adjective... as in venetian blind.'

Carlo darted another sharp look, but it was momentary. I suspect that he was thinking that, if anyone should win bonus points, better that it should be his treasured daughter than me, so he graciously gave way. 'So it is... Well done, darling!'

Theresa lifted the letters as she totted her score. There were two pink Double Word Scores. 'Eleven times four, forty-four. Plus a bonus of thirty. Seventy-eight!'

'Gosh. Well done, well done!' Carlo was pleased for his daughter, his pride trumping the competitive spirit he clearly possessed. And he had his own moment of satisfaction as he laid an 'X' down on a Triple Letter Score to make the word EXILE: twenty-eight points.

Theresa narrowly won the game, and I came a long way behind father and daughter, probably for the best. When Carlo said it was time for his bed, he kissed Theresa with a hug and shook me rather formally by the hand, but there was a glimmer of warmth, almost a twinkle, in his eyes as he wished me a good night's sleep.

*

The next day I took them both out to a pub for Sunday lunch before Theresa and I headed back to London. I had found the morning session with Carlo frustrating. Amongst the untidy shelves in the study was one full of books about culture and cultural studies, some of which were specifically about the cultural revolution of the 1960s. When I had asked Carlo if I could borrow two or three of these – I would take good care of them – the suspicious, defensive look had immediately veiled his eyes. He had refused the request, unconvincingly saying he needed them. He still had work to do on them.

When I asked if he had any photograph albums he nodded. 'Of the '60s?' I wondered.

A curt no. 'I didn't have a camera. Very few people did. There wasn't felt to be the same need then as there is now. Theresa is always showing me pictures she's taken on her phone. Hundreds and hundreds. I don't understand why!' But he did have some photos. He picked up a framed photo from his desk showing the chancellor of his university presenting him with a Waterford vase as a retirement present. He smiled as he showed it to me and it was the same strikingly lovely smile as his daughter's, open and inviting and joyous.

'You know, I think the progress of photography over the last fifty years is fascinating. When cameras became cheap – think of the Kodak Brownie, for example – they became accessible to more people. But film and developing were still expensive, so photographs were taken sparingly, judiciously. But then the big processing laboratories started developing more cheaply and offering replacement film as part of the deal. And that was the beginning of what I would call the Tyranny of Image.' I nodded. It was so good to hear Carlo talking in this relaxed manner about something that interested him. 'Since then every big occasion, every part of a holiday has needed to be captured, to be documented, and the taking of the photo has often become more important than the experience itself… And then phones with cameras came along and people now take thousands of pictures, most of which they will never look at. I call it the Tyranny of Image because we are slaves to the image, not the thing itself. And in the process we have lost the immediate experience, the primary experience. I mean, just think of those tourists – they're not all Japanese or Chinese, by the way! – who go into St Paul's, for example, or watch the Queen processing to open Parliament: they spend the whole time behind the lens. And all they see is the diminished image through the viewfinder or screen of a phone. They miss what they are actually there for.'

'Yes, it's crazy, isn't it!'

'And don't get me started on the selfie… Or the selfie-stick!' He exhaled a noisy, half-amused, half-irritated grunt of exasperation, before smiling benignly.

Now, as those eyes shone openly, as that mouth relaxed welcomingly, now was the time to ask him if we could arrange for some more meetings, for a series of interviews – about his academic life, about his influence in the 1960s. The smile disappeared instantly. 'Look, Theresa interviewed me a few years ago. It was fairly basic stuff, but I did give her very full answers to her questions… I don't know if she still has the tapes—'

'She does. She told me.'

'Well, perhaps you can use those if you are determined to go ahead with this unnecessary book. My memories there will be more reliable than anything I try to recall now. I am getting very forgetful these days. Theresa's probably told you.'

*

Driving back, I confessed to Theresa that I was very unsure about the project. Her father's reluctance to co-operate was greater than I had expected. I stressed how difficult it was to work with people who didn't want their stories told; how that was not the same as people being reticent or inarticulate; that my starting point with all the subjects I had worked with was that they had always at the very least wanted some story out there.

Her face spoke disappointment. 'I did warn you that he might be awkward. And it is, as you suggested on the journey down, a question of winning trust… Have you ever had to abandon projects you've already begun?'

'Sure,' I said. 'But I've not really even begun this one. Not really agreed to it yet. I haven't even discussed it with my agent. But sure, I've abandoned projects. Some years back I agreed to ghost the life of a well-known politician, a larger-than-life character who was much loved by the public. Man born into working-class poverty, left school at fourteen, worked in a shoe factory, became a councillor in his late twenties and eventually an MP, hugely popular, and adored by the media. I thought it would be a doddle, that the material would flow and that I simply would have to capture the man's voice. But it soon became clear, once I started doing some background research, that there was at least the possibility of an extremely unsavoury side to the man—'

'What sort of unsavoury?'

'Sexual. Children.'

'Yuk.'

'I told him that I had come across some stories about him, allegations. "Stuff and nonsense," he said. And he laughed them off and said that people in the public eye were always having accusations thrown at them. But there was something about him that made me uneasy, just a hunch on my part, I guess, so I told my agent that I didn't want to proceed... I had to pay back a sizeable publisher's advance – which fortunately I hadn't touched at that early stage – but I was happy to do that. I'm not really a believer in hagiography, anyway, but I certainly didn't want to risk whitewashing a rather sordid man, however great his achievements in public life.'

'Well, I can assure you that Papa does not have any skeletons in the closet,' she said with a laugh.

She talked about her childhood. About long summer days on the beach, about exhausting walks in the Purbeck hills, about the great care her father had always taken to ensure a happy and stable childhood for her and her brother. 'You know, he said to me once, when I was older, "The day your mother was taken from us, I knew that I had to be both father and mother to you both." And he has always looked after us wonderfully.' With the New Forest heathland stretching away on each side of the road, I could imagine the expansiveness of her childhood with her spoiling father trying so hard to be both parents to his bereaved children.

Eventually we joined the slow-moving traffic of west London and I dropped her back to Hammersmith. We had decided that the next stage was for me to listen to the tapes of her interviews with her father. I told her that she must give me time. I had a living to earn and so I must spend time on other projects.

She grabbed my hand, squeezed it hard and said, 'But please, Nick, please try to be as quick as you can. His mind is going, you know that. We don't have all the time in the world.'

I told her I'd do what I could. And drove back to Kingston feeling somewhat burdened. But not wholly burdened. I also felt a strange lightness, a hint of something exciting beginning to unfold.

3

It was time to write another entry for my blog. The fact that Theresa had said she enjoyed reading it had given me renewed interest in what at times had become something of a chore. I wanted to make use of my weekend in Dorset and wondered if I could post a piece offering advice on how to write about the countryside. What might be the starting points, the exercises one could suggest? I looked in an old, battered copy of *The South Country* by Edward Thomas to see if he had written about Dorset. I couldn't find anything, but there were several entries about neighbouring Hampshire. I was particularly struck by a piece about the decidedly unattractive chafer beetle, scourge of the well-kept lawn. Thomas's beetle, attracted by the light, has blundered indoors:

> He climbs, six-legged and slow, up the curtain, supporting himself now and then by unfurling his wings, or if not he falls with a drunken moan, then begins to climb again, and at last blunders about the room like a ball that must strike something, the

white ceiling, the white paper, the lamp, and when he falls he rests. In his painful climbing he looks human, as perhaps a man looks angelic to an angel; but there is nothing lovelier and more surprising than the unfurling of his pinions like a magic wind-blown cloak out of that hard mail.

I thought I would use this in my blog as an object lesson in writing about the natural world: the very precise observation, the careful use of simile, the imaginative and generous perspective. Taking the small, the ordinary, the unattractive even, and capturing it in words to offer a new and surprising way of perceiving it. I had my subject for my blog. I think – and maybe this was a thought that came to me much later – that at the back of my mind was also the notion of a creature finding itself in an alien environment, clumsy and out-of-place to begin with, before displaying its intrinsic nature. I wonder if somewhere was the subconscious thought of Carlo's transformations.

The blog's main purpose is to keep my name out there, to keep the work coming in and it is, therefore, written in my name, unlike most of my work. I have been asked on more than one occasion whether being a ghostwriter, where my identity remains hidden, gives me a diminished sense of self, a battered ego. Is it not extraordinarily frustrating, I am asked, to have a book in the best-seller lists and for no one to know that I have written it? I tell them that it is a question of expectation. I don't expect recognition, still less adulation, therefore am not disappointed when I don't get it.

The first-person narrative you are reading at the moment is actually (and unusually) me, Nick Barry. This is my story. Except that it is not, not really. It is Carlo's. Prince Carlo d'Abruzzi's.

*

I spent part of the morning listening to the first tape of Theresa's interviews with her father. This first required a hazardous trip to the unfloored attic, picking my way carefully along thin joists and ducking athletically under the cobwebbed rafter struts. After a search through various dusty, musty boxes, some containing stuff I didn't know I had and some with objects left behind by my departed wife, I finally retrieved my old cassette deck.

With a hope and a prayer, I plugged it into my hi-fi system. There was a hissing as the tape began and then a click and, 'It's on, I think... Yes, the light is blinking... So, Papa, let's start at the beginning. Where were you born?' The voice is girlish and slightly self-conscious.

'I was born in Trieste shortly before the Second World War. It had been a vibrant place for many years... A melting pot for various ethnic groups. They got along fine with each other... but tensions were stirred when the Germans began to influence things in Northern Italy. Trieste became a fractured place—'

'Tell me about your parents, Papa. They both died young, didn't they?'

'Yes, they did... My mother, Maria, a beautiful woman by all accounts, married my father Umberto when she was very young. He was a fine man who had fought bravely in the First World War and was decorated. He fought with the Royal Italian Army, for the Allied side, of course. I don't remember my mother at all. She died when I was very young… and in 1940 my father was killed in a plane crash. I was six at the time. My nanny had friends in England, and thought it best that we leave Italy and live with them. They kindly took me in and brought me up in Devon.'

I was alarmed at the similarity of this account to what Carlo had told me at the weekend. I wasn't worried about the content. That of course would be the same. But the similarity of the wording bothered me. I made a note to ask Theresa when the first signs of her father's dementia had appeared. The tape was, I estimated, seven or eight years old.

Carlo reminisces on life in Devon. He talks about his schooling. Being teased for his accent, quickly learning English, begging his foster mother to help him with the language every evening. He talks about her kindness, about trying to repay the kindness by helping on the smallholding that she and her husband farmed. There is warmth in the sonorous baritone voice, a deep affection for his foster parents.

'Did you never think of going back to Trieste after the war?' Theresa asks.

'No. There was nothing for me there. No one for me.'

'What about the other branches of the family? Uncles, aunts, cousins?' There is a long silence. 'Papa?'

'No.' Another long pause. 'My father broke all his ties with his family when he married my mother.'

'Is that why I have never met any uncles and aunts, any cousins, Papa? I must have some.'

The voice has lost its composure, has become crackly. 'Yes… But I lost all contact a very long time ago.'

There is the sound of clothing being brushed, of Carlo trying to clear his throat. Theresa is perhaps embracing her father, trying to offer some comfort. She says nothing, but I could sense the pain, the sympathy she felt for her uprooted, isolated father. I decided to leave the tape for the time being. In any case, it was time to eat.

*

I had arranged to meet George Nelson for a pub lunch. George was a very successful paparazzo who, over the years, had made a shedload of money from his celebrity shots. He was a rogue. He would have been the first to admit it, probably; but I suspected that he liked to regard himself as a loveable rogue. Certainly he had a chutzpah that could make one smile in disbelief, which I suppose is inevitable with real chutzpah. He could duck and weave his way in or out of any situation and spent much of his career doing just that. Much of the week he could be found driving around the smarter parts of London in search of his next pay cheque. He always carried with him a thick, grubby notebook of celebrity addresses, phone numbers and car registration plates to assist him in his constant quest for the must-have celebrity shot, the one that would start a bidding war between rival newspapers or magazines. He could make £3,000 from a dull, workaday sleb shot, but the money shot – the celebrity caught cheating on a partner, the lurid photo of a drunken night out, the beach shot revealing unsightly rolls of fat or stretch marks that no one suspected – these could fetch up to £30,000.

George was already seated when I arrived at the pub. There was a podgy solidity to him, both in body and head, the roundness of his face accentuated by the close cropping of what remained of his hair. The rotund face was rarely without a cheeky grin, the self-confident expression of a man who knew where he fitted in to a weird and wacky world.

He was on his feet as I walked over to the table. 'What's your poison, mate?' he asked in the broadest of cockney. I always suspected that the accent was adopted or, at the very least, exaggerated: part of the persona he had created of a cheeky chappie, a diamond geezer; an antidote to the largely sleazy nature of his work. But behind the superficial twinkle in his eyes, the spark of a naughty mischief-making boy, lay something else, an opaqueness that suggested something private and hidden.

He had summoned me because he wanted a piece written about him that he could tout around the weekend magazines, and he thought I might be the ideal fit to translate him from the odium of the reprobate to the esteem of the reputable. I can't think why. We both worked with celebrities but, whereas I was invited into their lives, he sneaked in unasked and unwanted, thieving their privacy. On the other hand, I was a wordsmith-for-hire, and I thought it would be slightly precious of me not even to listen to his proposal.

I asked him what he had been up to lately. He had been in Cornwall, he told me. I'd be surprised, he said, how many famous people took to the fresh and revivifying airs and waters of the West Country. But his real mission had been to snoop around the locations of a continuing drama series that was currently in production. Either of its two major stars, caught off guard, would offer the possibility of a high-value photo.

'But to business, me ol' mate. I wanna get a bit of quality coverage that paints a good picture of me, something in one of the broadsheet weekend supplements – *Times*, *Telegraph*, *Observer*, that kind of thing. Something kosher. Thing is I can't keep up this malarkey forever. Perched on the back of a speeding motorbike, squeezed into some thorny bush, lying low in a stinking ditch for hours. I'd like to become a photojournalist, something more respectable for me old age. Do proper stuff. So I want to begin to clean up me image. And you're the geezer to do the right stuff. The write stuff. Ha ha! Geddit?'

I smiled, weakly I imagine. 'You're asking me to polish a turd, are you?'

He laughed very loudly at this. 'Yes, mate! You got it.' He guffawed some more. 'Polish a turd! Love it!'

'I'm sure that there are plenty of journalists, freelancers and staffers who would be very happy to write an article on you.'

'Nah, I don't want nobody else writing about me. *I* want to write an article about me. Then I'll be in control of what's said… So I need a ghost. I need you, mate.'

I told him I wasn't sure. I'd have to think about it and would get back to him. If I was up for the job, we could sketch out some ideas and then I'd interview him.

We were about to order lunch when his phone went. He listened, barked an abrupt, 'Got it,' and rose from the table, saying to me, 'I gotta scoot. See ya, mate. Let me know soon.' And he was gone, presumably to prey on another poor, unsuspecting sleb. I could understand why he might want to settle down. The strange rhythm of his life could hardly be good for his health – the frenetic chasing and, in contrast, the long stake-outs that required the patience of a fisherman before he made his catch.

*

When I got home, I went back to the tape. Theresa had obviously stopped recording when her father had become upset. The new section was about his happy days on the farm. Learning to shear sheep. There were some amusing tales of his early attempts. He makes Theresa laugh with descriptions of mangled sheep who look like the victims of a demon barber; and of the time he yanked a sheep up on to its hind legs to shear underneath, lost his balance and ended up on his back with the sheep on top of him.

And then Theresa asks him, foolishly perhaps, if he has any memories at all of Trieste. His voice cracks with emotion. 'Not really…But I do remember the kitchen of our apartment. I can picture the room clearly, every last detail of it. The colour of the cupboards, the crockery, the scrubbed stove… And I remember my nanny taking me into town to see my father—' And then he starts to cry and the tape is switched off.

4

The next day I got a call from Theresa asking if I was free on Saturday evening. I said, teasingly, that I could be if I were to get a good enough offer. She wanted me to go round for dinner to meet her brother, Luca. I suspected the real intention behind the invitation was to keep the pressure on me to push on with the tapes. I accepted the dinner date.

I decided it was time to call Vikki, my agent. I told her about Carlo, about the various pies he had a finger in during the sixties. I told her my plan was to centre the narrative of the proposed book on Carlo's life in the sixties, radiating out from his various involvements to give a sort of social history of the decade, with a special focus on the revolution in popular culture. She was interested; thought she could place it. She asked me to write the opening chapter and a chapter synopsis as soon as I was ready.

I continued listening to Theresa's interviews of her father, taking notes where appropriate, listing questions for either her or Carlo. At the age of seventeen he went to university, not in the UK as might be expected after his English education, but in America, at Columbia, where he took a Liberal Arts degree. He speaks with great fondness of his days in New York. 'Happy, happy days, they were, Theresa. It was such a different culture for me. Busy, colourful. And I was amongst people at Columbia that I could hardly have imagined from my Devon schooldays… And New York was so exciting, so cosmopolitan. You could see why everything good in the world was coming out of America.'

He then talks about his year at sea. The roughness of the sailors, the fear and excitement of passing through ferocious storms, the foreign ports with exotic attractions. 'New York was so different from Devon. And then the sea was so different again. I felt I was growing in different ways.' He tells his daughter how important books were, of his eclectic reading, of how Conrad's *Youth* had sent him to sea.

However, the real life-changer, he says, came in the clubs of Hamburg, where he was witnessing a new kind of music that was unlike anything he'd heard in America. He speaks warmly of the thrusting vitality of the reconstructed city, the optimism of the new Germany, the enthusiastic embrace of modernity. But the deepest excitement in his voice, as Theresa throws in the occasional and probably unnecessary prompt, is that reserved for the Beatles.

'The leathers they wore were probably inspired by America, and most of the music, too, I guess, had its origins across the Pond, but the sound, the sound was new, quite new. The rawness, the roughness, owed nothing to the Americans, but to the peculiarities of the Scouse accent with its harsh, throaty, phlegmy scratch, its bubbling amalgam of Lancashire and Ireland; the jaggedness of the sound came from something stripped back and essential in the musicianship of the band.' There is an interesting contrast between the voices he is describing and the golden richness of his own voice. 'They were young men who were primarily trying to please themselves. As far as they were concerned, it didn't matter if other people liked or disliked it, they could take it or leave it.'

'Interesting,' Theresa chips in.

'There was a swagger and defiance in them, softened perhaps by a rather childish wit. And I knew, I just knew, that I was witnessing a whole new generational outlook. And to be honest, who could blame the forward-looking people of Hamburg for taking to this dishevelled but musically well-drilled band? To me it was no surprise that they should flourish in this edgy city.'

He tells Theresa about his decision to abandon the sea; he will sign up to one last passage as a sailor to ensure arrival in Liverpool. On a new cassette tape he describes his trek from the docks, on a gloomy November morning to meet Brian Epstein in his record shop. The detail is as fresh in his mind as if he were describing the events of the day before. He speaks of Epstein with great affection. He senses immediately that he has come to the right man, that it is Epstein who has the energy and the vision to bring the Beatles to the world. He talks with sadness about the Epstein he visited six years later to complain of his omission from the *Sergeant Pepper* collage. The man is wrecked, defeated. He will shortly be dead.

*

I made notes as I listened to the tapes and very quickly was able to write a first chapter for my proposed book that I could bang off to my agent as a sample. My focus was Epstein and I framed the chapter with Carlo's 1961 and 1967 visits to him. With the clarity and the vividness of detail provided by the tape, the chapter had pretty much written itself, give or take one or two Google checks for spellings, for old photos of 1960s Liverpool and for a quick Street View zoom through the relevant parts of the city so that I could picture Carlo's journey in my own mind. Fact-checking and a fleshing out of the detail could come later. My provisional title for the project was *Catalysing the Counter Culture*.

Vikki rang me back on the Friday afternoon. She liked what she had read and was looking forward to seeing a full synopsis. 'I've not heard of d'Abruzzi before, I have to say, but he sounds very interesting. And I love the lineage! The royal and Napoleonic background adds a layer of exoticism which I think you should explore a little more.'

*

BEGINNINGS

It is a drab November morning in 1961. Wet pavements mirror the greyness of the day as the people of Liverpool make their way to work. Their dull clothing, the long dark coats, the muted tones of the women's hats and headscarves, adds to the drabness of the scene. But amongst these dreary crowds a distinctive figure might catch the eye, the figure of a striking young man. His shoes look expensive – Italian perhaps – his trousers are tight-fitting, and his hair is on the longish side, unfashionably so. He has made his way from the docks, where he has disembarked from a freighter, bringing to a close his short career as a merchant seaman.

Our one-time sailor is Carlo d'Abruzzi, and Carlo d'Abruzzi – though he has never told his fellow sailors this – is a prince. He is a prince descended from the kings of Italy – Bonapartes, too, to add lustre to his pedigree. He is a prince who is about to become a catalysing force behind what will become the Swinging Sixties. Some would say – simplistically, no doubt – that he was indeed the primum mobile of the cultural revolution that lifted the grey gloom of the post-war years.

Our man was in Hamburg earlier in the year. Like Liverpool, the German port too was smashed to pieces from the air. Unlike Liverpool, it has risen from its destruction with a quickness and energy that has astonished; a strange premium for the losing side in a punishing war. Liverpool continues its slow recovery, and many parts of the city are still convalescent. In the centre, important civic buildings have been repaired and restored, and the gaps between the surviving grander buildings have been infilled with plain, rectangular structures built cheaply in the modern post-war idiom.

On this dull November morning, there is no disguising the shabbiness of the city. But something is astir. There is a bright incipience in the air, a glow that lends a gentle incandescence to the morning fog. Soon it will blaze into a febrile excitement that will reverberate across the country and then across the globe.

Carlo d'Abruzzi turns from the Strand into James Street. As he walks past the former White Star building he pauses for a moment to admire its fine brick and stonework. The elaborate Queen Anne style suggests the confidence of a vanished age, of a time when Liverpool was one of the busiest and wealthiest ports in the world.

Church Street is abustle. Crowds of people mill along the pavements and cross the road in great swarms; a few cars weave carefully through the masses, and buses in groups of three of four inch their way across the city. D'Abruzzi stops for a moment at Woolworths to buy himself a jotter pad. Who knows what notes he'll need to take after his important meeting?

He is on a mission. He knows who he wants to see. He believes he can change the life of this man. And he believes that his own life, too, is on the cusp of change, is about to open into a new and wonderful adventure. He carries with him a gift, a slender object seven inches square wrapped in a brown paper bag. If his hunch is correct, this object will transform the life of the man he is about to meet, will alter the lives of the people of Liverpool; this spinning object will radiate into millions of households, he believes.

He has turned back along Church Street and now is turning right into Whitechapel where he quickly finds the shop he is looking for. Above the elaborate window display, emblazoned in large modern lettering, is the name of the shop: NEMS.

He enters, walks up to a counter and asks the girl who is standing behind boxes of records if he can see Mr Epstein. She pops into one of the listening booths and out promptly steps a very smartly dressed young man. He wears a dark, well-cut suit, a white shirt and a thin blue tie. He smiles warmly at Carlo. 'How can I help you, sir?' he asks.

'I was wondering, Mr Epstein, if you had heard this.' He hands over the brown paper bag he has been carrying.

It contains a 7" record which Epstein takes from its sleeve. The writing on the orange label is in German, apart from the title of the song and the name of the performing band. '*My Bonnie.* Tony Sheridan and The Beats... No, I'm not familiar with this. I've heard of Tony Sheridan... but The Beats? No.'

'Actually it's the Beatles. A Liverpool band who have been working in Germany.

But they are back here now. In Liverpool.'

Epstein takes the record to one of the many turntables in the shop and invites Carlo into a listening booth. After a slow first verse traditionally sung, there is an eruption into a high-octane rendition of the rest of the song, driven by a pulsating guitar and emphatic, frenzied drumming. Epstein's face breaks into a broad smile. 'I like it!' he says.

Carlo's excitement, which has been contained on his walk to the shop, now spills into a jabbering monologue. 'They're fabulous. Hamburg clubs. Indra. Kaiserkeller. Top Ten. Star-Club. Fabulous music. They play for hours. R&B, blues, rock and roll. Raw, raucous. You've got to see them. They're here now. They're back. You've gotta see them. The Cavern... Just... real. Real music. Fabulous. We'll go together.'

Epstein has been smiling patiently. 'I would like to hear them.' Carlo nods vigorously. 'But why have you come to me about them?'

'I was told that that you had the best record shop in Liverpool and that if you stocked the record and ordered the band's LP you would bring them to the attention of a wider audience.'

A slow nod from Epstein. 'The Cavern?' he says. 'Mathew Street. Just round the corner. Three-minute walk. When are they next playing there?'

'Today! Lunch time!'

'All right, let's do it. Come back here at midday and we'll pop along.'

Carlo spends the next couple of hours wandering around the city centre, reflecting on the man he has just met. He likes him. There is a freshness, an openness, a straightforwardness that is endearing. There is a boyish, toothy, charming smile. And the voice: much posher than Carlo had expected.

As they walk towards the Cavern Club they chat. Carlo tells Epstein that he has been to sea looking for adventure. 'In my final year at university I read Joseph Conrad's *Youth*. My friends had all been reading Kerouac's *On the Road* and were planning great road trips. But for me it was the sea. So I signed on. And I've had a great year. And now, I think, I'm ready for land again. What about you? Any great adventures?'

'Well, yes, actually. I went to London to become an actor. But that didn't work out. And then my father put me to work in the record shop. And it's gone very well. Very well. But to be honest, I'm getting a little bored with it now.'

An actor. That would explain the voice, thinks Carlo. He tells Epstein about the vibrancy of Hamburg, the bright lights and the louche people to be found on the Reeperbahn.

They arrive in Mathew Street. It is

narrow. Tall, dirty buildings rise up either side of them. The two men enter the scruffy frontage of the Cavern Club and are directed to the basement. It is dark and dank and smoky. Amongst the tightly packed crowd there is an air of expectancy.

The band strolls on stage. Epstein looks with mild distaste at the way they are dressed: black leathers, black shirts or crew tops. They look scruffy, dishevelled. But when they start to play his expression is transformed into astonishment. There is raw energy and a strong rhythmic pulse to which, Carlo notices, Epstein is moving his body rather awkwardly, stiffly and just a little out of sync with the beat. As songs come to an end there is banter between the members of the band and between the band and the audience.

By the time the set concludes, there is the broadest of beams on Epstein's face. 'They're tremendous. As you say, fabulous. I'm surprised I haven't heard them before. Thank you. Thank you for bringing me here. Look, let me take you out for lunch by way of recompense. I know a nice place in Hackins Hey.'

Over lunch the animated talk is mainly about the band, the strangely named Beatles. Carlo says the sound is completely new and will take the younger generation by storm, will be bigger than Bill Haley, bigger than Elvis, even. Epstein wonders, and asks Carlo whether he should approach the Beatles and offer to manage them.

*

Five and a half years later Carlo d'Abruzzi is once again walking to meet Brian Epstein. Once again he carries a record, an album on this occasion. Carlo cuts a colourful figure on this bright June morning, but he does not stand out from the crowd. London has become a delirium of colour, of noise, of brash confidence since the grey dullness of the early 1960s. Carlo wears maroon velvet trousers, a geometrically patterned blue and white shirt, and his long hair frames a fashionable moustache which curves around the sides of his mouth. The cheerfulness of the outward appearance does not match the inner mood of the man. He is once more on a mission, but this time he wants an explanation.

He mounts the four steps to the door of 24 Chapel Street and rings the bell. There is a long pause before someone appears, Epstein's personal assistant Joanne Petersen, presumably. He tells her he has come to see her boss and she leads him to a study on the first floor, saying Mr Epstein will be with him shortly.

It is a while before Epstein appears and when he does Carlo is shocked. The man looks dreadful. He is fuller in the face these days, but sickly looking, and the eyes have lost their openness, the directness of gaze that Carlo remembers.

'Carlo.' The voice is quiet, and toneless, the outstretched hand a little shaky.

'Brian! How are you?' Carlo peers at him quizzically. 'Are you okay? You don't look well.'

'A little over-indulgence last night, perhaps... I'm fine.' But the voice is listless and the eyes downcast. 'Why have you come to see me?'

'About this.' He takes the album out of a carrier bag, the brilliant colours catching a beam of sunlight. '*Sgt. Pepper.*' Carlo realises he is sounding querulous but cannot help himself. He stabs his finger at the front cover of the album, demanding Epstein's attention. The finger is landing on an unidentifiable figure in a red and yellow striped bonnet, a hairdresser's dummy. To her left, mostly hidden, is an image of James Joyce, above Bob Dylan and below Lawrence of Arabia. 'What the hell is this? I was supposed to be here. Peter Blake told me I would be on the cover. In recognition of discovering the Beatles. In recognition of all I've done since.'

'Carlo, look, I'm sorry, but it's really nothing to do with me. You'll have to talk to Peter, or to John... I haven't been much involved this year. They don't tour anymore and for months they've been cooped up in

the recording studio with George Martin...
I can't help you. I'm sorry.' There is a deep
sadness in his voice; he sounds desolate, on
the verge of tears.

They talk a little. Epstein explains that
he is thinking of selling his company, NEMS
Enterprises. He seems to have lost all
confidence, lost all his boyish optimism; the
man seems very, very tired. There doesn't
appear to be much point in staying, so
Carlo gently squeezes Epstein's arm, says
his goodbyes and leaves, walking out into a
sunlit Belgravia.

He takes the tube at Hyde Park Corner,
changes lines at Leicester Square and
heads northwards to Chalk Farm, to the
Roundhouse. He has arranged to meet people
there who he hopes will allow him to hire
the wonderful old railway shed. He wants to
promote a concert with Jim Morrison and
The Doors. He likes the venue, its Victorian
brick solidity, its paradoxical sense of both
spaciousness and intimacy. He was there a
year earlier for the launch of *International
Times*, an underground magazine of which
he was a co-founder. He wants the concert to
be an all-night affair and he knows that this
will not be possible at the Albert Hall where,
two years earlier, he helped to organise
the International Poetry Incarnation with
Allen Ginsberg. That night remains one of
his most vivid memories: the sweet smell of
dope, the brash informality in this elegant

Victorian memorial building, the sense that the excited, noisy celebration of new values marked a changing of the guard.

Carlo d'Abruzzi was a big man in the 1960s. By his own admission he was the chief architect of the Counter Culture, the man who blew away the grey clouds of 1950s post-war Britain, who unshackled the arts from the stylistic stringencies of the establishment, who liberated a generation from the stifling orthodoxies of a moribund morality. Prince Carlo d'Abruzzi.

5

Luca was already at Theresa's flat when I arrived for dinner. Tall and wiry, he was not very similar to his twin. He had brown eyes whereas she had blue and, unlike her, he had inherited his father's Roman nose, with its high bridge and pronounced curve; in fact, the shape of his face and his hair were very like his father's.

He smiled warmly and held out a hand. 'Hi, I'm Luca. I've heard quite a bit about you from Theresa, Nick,' he said.

'Excellent!' I replied. 'I'm looking forward to getting to know you both. And your father, of course.'

There was perhaps just a slight weakening of his smile as I mentioned his father. Probably, like Theresa, he worried about the incipient dementia.

While Theresa withdrew to the kitchen and Nick went to get me a drink, I looked around the sitting room, which I had not seen when I had lunched with her previously. It was like a thousand front rooms in small basement flats. A bay window, a Victorian fireplace filled with a display of dried flowers, a door to the narrow hall passageway. The furnishings were simple and tasteful, unremarkable apart from a corner table that seemed to be something of a shrine to Theresa's father. A carefully arranged group of frames contained photographs of Carlo at various ages. The most striking was the only one which showed him as a young man.

'I'm guessing this is 1965, the Poetry Incarnation at the Albert Hall,' I said to Luca as he returned with my drink.

Luca nodded. 'Yes. I think Theresa would tell you it is one of her most prized possessions.'

The photograph was taken from behind a rostrum on which a poet – I didn't recognise who – was reading. Beyond the rostrum was the audience, uniformly young, casually dressed, attentive. And there, in the second row, unmistakably was Carlo, smoking what might have been a cigarette or might have been a joint.

'Your father helped organise the event, didn't he?' I asked.

'So I gather,' said Luca. He spoke with a curious lack of enthusiasm or pride.

At that moment Theresa entered the room. 'All going well! I'm free for the moment. Do sit down, Nick.'

Luca was in the only armchair, leaving me and Theresa to the sofa. The movement of air as she sat down beside me released a draught of sweet fragrance. 'I was just looking at the photo of the Albert Hall event,' I said.

'Ah yes, it's brilliant, isn't it?'

'Absolutely! …How did your dad come to arrange such a huge and historic event?'

'Well. Allen Ginsberg was over earlier in the month – June, I think it was – for a reading somewhere in the Charing Cross Road, and Papa suggested to him that it would be good to do reading at a bigger venue. When Allen asked him what the biggest venue in London was, Papa said the Albert Hall. "Would you like me to book it for you?" he asked. Allen said he sure would! And that he might be able to get some of his fellow beat poets such as Gregory Corso and Lawrence Ferlinghetti along. And that's what happened. I think something like fifteen poets did readings. Brilliant! Quite brilliant!'

We talked inconsequentially for a while and then she asked Luca to help bring the table out from the bay window and lay it up for the meal. As she disappeared back into the kitchen, I thought I'd ask Luca about his work. I knew that he was a lawyer. He'd taken an English degree before doing a Law Conversion course and joining a firm that specialised in media law.

'Is it interesting work?' I asked.

'Well… Mostly not. Contracts, and that kind of dull stuff. But it can get interesting occasionally! What about you, Nick? You must get to meet all kinds of fascinating people in your line of work.'

Theresa returned with the starters. 'Fascinating people? Who are you talking about?' she asked.

'Nick was just about to tell me about all the interesting celebs he meets through his work.'

'Celebs. Slebs! "Celebrity" is strange concept, isn't it? A kind of dilution of the fame that in ages past people had to earn.'

'Oh? Is that true?' Luca asked. 'Actually, I think most celebrities today have some talent or quality – short-lived, possibly – that endows them with a charisma of some kind. I don't think the modern cult of celebrity is very different from notions of fame in the past. David Beckham, Benedict Cumberbatch, they are both talented practitioners of their crafts. The Duke of Wellington was a talented strategist and leader of men… They're just different subsets of the same thing: fame… Which in any case you could argue is never ever fully deserved… is often randomly or fortuitously conferred. I would argue that fame has always been dependent on the same things; on a combination of social background, performance… projected visibility. And plain, old-fashioned luck.'

Theresa was looking at Luca with an admiring smile; and then at me expectantly, waiting for the rally.

'Subset. Yes. Yes, I suppose you're right. And actually, when people talk about the emptiness of celebrity – the lack of genuine merit that often accompanies modern celebrity – they forget that it is not so different from the old status systems of the past. Which would depend on matters of age, gender, your parents' status, ethnicity and, as you say, plain luck.'

'Exactly,' said Luca.

'I mean, kings and queens… princes… have, for example, typically been the most famous members of their generation, and have usually simply inherited their position… with no guarantee of their talent, or merit or quality, still less charisma. And that is little different today. For goodness' sake, just look at Charles!'

Theresa laughed and looked at Luca for a response. 'True. And I suppose you could say that Paris Hilton – often a butt of ridicule and often cited as an example of the emptiness of modern celebrity – is perhaps not significantly different from Princess Di. Both were born to high-status families of real past achievement, and both were beautiful, sexy, rich women who had the cachet to enter effortlessly into the glittering world of socialites.'

A nodding of heads, a pouring of more wine by Luca, a clearing of plates, and it was time for the main course. The crab and avocado starter was followed by a beef and ale stew. Theresa was undoubtedly a talented cook, and I complimented her efforts.

She smiled. 'I'm so glad you're enjoying it!' Warmed by the wine, I thought how easy it would be to fall in love with that young face, with its perfect, unblemished skin, its wide, honest eyes, its perfectly curved lips that were slightly and enticingly parted.

Luca had asked me about celebrities and I wondered what kind of contact he had with them, working for a media law firm. 'You must come into contact with slebs,' I suggested.

'Occasionally. Normally not very edifying. A couple of years ago we had to obtain a super-injunction for... well, let's give him his legal name – CTF – who really was quite an unsavoury character. I don't know if you remember the case. Some paparazzo had photographed him in a threesome. Not unusual, but in this case the ingredients of the sex sandwich were rather extraordinary. CTF was the filling, with a sixteen-year-old girl beneath him and her seventeen-year-old brother on top bumming him.'

'Oh my word!' I said. 'It adds a new dimension to the phrase "gagging order"!'

Theresa giggled and then made a gagging sound. 'Spare us the detail, Luca!'

'I am pretty sure I know who the paparazzo was,' I volunteered, remembering that George Nelson had told me that this was one of the many scrapes he'd got into with the law.

'Oh, do tell us!'

'I can't, I'm afraid, Theresa. He's an old rogue. And I'm sure that he would feel duty-bound to eliminate both of us if he thought I had shared my secret with you!'

'Spoily sport. No pudding for you, then!' She grinned teasingly. 'Only kidding.' She got up to clear the dishes away and collect the desserts.

'Actually,' said Luca, 'there is a very interesting legal view on the commodification of celebrity… with the intriguing question: who owns celebrity? There are, after all, multiple creators – the celebrity himself, the 'team' behind that person and importantly, of course, the public who confer the celebrity status. It's a tricky area. Some lawyers would argue that celebrities should not be granted exclusive rights to their own images.'

'Wow! That's really interesting. I'd never thought about it like that before now.' Theresa was thinking this through.

There was something of a hiatus in the conversation as attention was drawn to the pudding of a rich chocolate mousse. And then Luca began a new rumination.

'You know, I think that chance – chance in the sense of lucky visibility – is the most interesting aspect of celebrity. For example, the singer who croons with a fabulous baritone voice, but only ever in the shower, will never be famous. He's like one of the unsung heroes in Gray's country churchyard. Like "Some mute inglorious Milton…".'

'You've got a wonderful voice, Luca. It's a shame so few people hear it!' And it suddenly struck me that Luca's voice, his speaking voice, had that same baritone richness of his father's.

A look of sadness had clouded Theresa's face.

'Hearing you talk about unsung heroes makes me think of Papa. Of how few people know of his achievements.' She looked and sounded close to tears. 'It makes me so sad that he is gradually losing his memory and maybe will fade away without ever receiving, hearing, the recognition he deserves.'

'But that's what I'm here to change!' I told her. She nodded enthusiastically, the sad face banished. 'And when Luca talks about chance, isn't that exactly what your father illustrates? Being in Hamburg at exactly the right time!' Another enthusiastic nod.

'I'll go and get some coffee.'

As she was clattering around in the kitchen, Luca touched my arm and spoke in a quiet voice, almost a whisper. 'Look, you must be careful with Tease—'

'Tease?'

'Oh, sorry. Theresa... Tease. It's what I've called her since we were tiny little children... Theresa worships her father – our father – and is setting a huge store on her – your – project. You need to proceed carefully. Cautiously. I'd hate for her to get hurt.'

I was wondering if Luca had got into his head the idea that I had set my sights on Theresa, that I was hoping for a sexual adventure, which of course I was not. But as he continued, I realised that was not the nature of his concern. 'The thing is, Dad can get very carried away with his stories. You know, he exaggerates. Embroiders. I just think you need to be aware of that. Keep it in mind as you proceed.'

I nodded, and at that moment Theresa returned with the coffee.

'I liked your brother a lot,' I told her. 'Really interesting to talk to.'

'Good! I like him, too! My little bro!'

'Little? You're twins!'

'He was born fourteen minutes after me. So. Little bro!'

We were sitting together on the sofa. Luca had gone home and Theresa had waylaid my attempt at leave-taking by entreating me to have one for the road. The measure of whisky she poured 'for the road' was so excessive that it made any prospect of driving home hazardous, to say nothing of illegal.

When I told her this, she said, 'So? I can make up the sofa bed for you.'

So I stayed.

These decisions are often a mistake, with complications unforeseen in the alcoholic glow of contentment, and this would turn out to be a wrong move. Or the lack of the right move.

Theresa talked excitedly about the belated fame the project would bring her father; about how lucky she was to have found me to push the project forward; about her passionate hope that the film rights to Carlo's story would be snapped up by someone very quickly.

'It's such a good story. The escape from Trieste, the idyllic childhood in Devon; the travel. And then the whirlwind decade when he discovers the Beatles, promotes the Beat Poets and The Doors, and the rest of it.'

Unwisely, she had poured refills for both our whisky glasses. She was not drunk, but there was slight sibilant slurring to her speech. Mainly, however, it was a voice spilling over with excitement. 'I've thought about how one might structure the film,' she said. 'The main narrative could be him teaching at uni, teaching his Cultural Studies seminars, and intercut with this in appropriate places would be flashbacks telling the story of his past. What do you think?'

There was a look of eagerness on her face, defying contradiction. It seemed unkind to dampen her enthusiasm, but I felt I had to temper it somewhat. 'Theresa, slow down a little! We must take it one step at a time. Do the research. Get a publisher. Write the book!' I briefly put my hand over hers as I said this, to reassure her that I was not being critical.

Suddenly, out of nowhere she exclaimed in an over-loud voice, 'Tell me about your wife!'

'What?'

'Tell me about your wife!'

'Why?'

'What was her name?'

I stared at her in disbelief.

She leant towards me and pummelled my chest gently. 'What was her name?'

'Helen.'

'And why did Helen leave you? …She must have been mad!' I don't think this was a conscious attempt at flirtation, but her eyes were wide and inviting, her pupils dilated.

I explained that she hadn't left me as such, we had split up. I told her about the footballer for whom I wrote a weekend column in one of the Sunday tabloids. About coming home one day to find him in bed with Helen.

'Whaat!' Her hand sprang instinctively to her mouth to stifle an emerging giggle.

'I know,' I said. 'I know it's got its comic side.'

'But why did she do it?'

'Well, from her point of view I can understand it. A last throw of the dice, perhaps, for someone on the threshold of middle age. And flattering, of course, to have this fit young man coming on to you, although, of course, it wasn't exactly *Match of the Day*… I guess she was just looking for a vigour she no longer found in me… But what puzzles me more is what was in it for him. Anything more than a momentary physical urge, an animal urge quickly satisfied, of no more significance than a quick wank?'

She giggled again as I said this. 'What was the name of the footballer? Would I have heard of him?'

'Probably. But I am not going to tell you.'

I interrupted her protests by saying it was time to get some sleep. 'Yes, yes,' she said, rising from the sofa a little unsteadily. 'I'll get some bedclothes.'

I could hear a rummaging in a cupboard in the hallway, and then she was back, instructing me to pull out the sofa bed, and asking me to help put the sheet on it. She wobbled as she bent down with a duvet, squawking and apologising for her unsteadiness.

She placed a light kiss on my lips and was off to her room.

*

At about two o'clock I needed to go for a pee. To get to the bathroom, which lay beyond the kitchen, I had to go past

Theresa's bedroom. Conscious of my nakedness and hoping to cause minimum disturbance, I decided not to click the light switch and instead to feel my way along the corridor. A tiny green LED light on a piece of kitchen equipment guided my way, and soon I had relieved myself, as noiselessly as possible. But as I made my way back along the corridor, I was aware of a dim light spilling from the bedroom. And in the next moment saw the moonlit silhouette of Theresa standing in the doorway.

'Are you okay?' she asked.

As I stopped and turned to her, instead of more naturally covering my exposed penis, I put my hands on her warm shoulders, bare apart from the thin shoulder straps of her nightdress. 'Yes. Just been for a wee.'

And in that moment, either she or I moved just a fraction forward, and there was a simultaneous embrace. I felt myself quickly hardening against the thin, soft material of her nightdress. Our mouths met and we stumbled, crablike, towards the bed.

There were few preliminaries. As I kissed her mouth and neck, she pulled her nightdress up to her waist and drew me into her, emitting a low grunt on my entry. I held back for as long as I was able to and, as I finished, her high, light, breathy murmurs deepened into a prolonged groan of satisfaction.

*

I awoke at about five o'clock. I lay on my back for some minutes, paralysed with a deepening dread at what I had done, before making my way quietly back to the sofa bed.

I couldn't get back to sleep. The sense of shame, the regret at having done what I had always promised myself I would never do, filled my head. Never ever sleep with a client had always been my rule. And now I would just have to live with the consequences of my foolish breach of that rule. I would need time to think things through properly, but it was unlikely I would be able to continue with the Carlo d'Abruzzi story.

At about seven o'clock I heard Theresa using the bathroom and a little later putting the kettle on in the kitchen. I quickly got dressed, cleared the bedding and restored the sofa to its primary function and position. The noise must have alerted Theresa. There was a knock on the door.

'Can I come in?' she asked breezily.

I grunted a 'Yes', hardly daring to look her in the eye when she entered.

'What would Big Boy like for breakfast?' she asked with a slight giggle.

'Look, Theresa, I'm sorry about what happened last night. It shouldn't have happened.'

'What? It was good!'

'No. It complicates the writer-client relationship. It shouldn't have happened, and it won't happen again if we continue with the project.'

'Oh, you old-fashioned thing, you!' she said, laughing. 'Don't worry about it. Regard it as a one-night stand, if you like, or a no-strings bonus for the excellent work you are doing on Papa.' I am not sure what expression she detected in my face, but she continued, somewhat shockingly in my view. 'Don't worry about it… What was it you said last night about the mysterious footballer and your ex? Something like, "It was an animal thing, of no more significance than a quick wank." Correct?'

I left Theresa, saying I had a busy day ahead and would skip breakfast. On the drive home I pondered the complications I had created. I liked Theresa, liked her brother, Luca, and was interested in the story of Carlo. I would need time to process just how damaging my one-night stand had been. It clearly was of no special significance or consequence to Theresa, who seemed to regard it with amused detachment.

6

I had agreed to take George Nelson's commission to write the autobiographical article that he would try to sell to a Sunday broadsheet. Who knew, perhaps I could 'polish the turd' to such a bright incandescence that the broadsheets would be clamouring for him in his new incarnation as a serious photojournalist. I was heading for his house in Chiswick with a view to making some preliminary notes. I had put the Carlo d'Abruzzi research on ice for a few days and had not spoken to Theresa.

I knew that George's work paid well, so it was no surprise to see that he had found himself an attractive three-storeyed terrace house in a pretty little street; small, well-maintained façades, front gardens imaginatively and expensively planted.

'Howdy doody, scribe!' he said as he opened the door. 'Enter the Papararium, home to the deadly fang-toothed snapper of East Chis Wick!' He gave a proprietorial grin and waved a hand expansively to beckon me in.

He let me into a large kitchen-living room that looked as though it had recently received a very expensive refit.

'What can I get yer? What's yer poison, mate?'

'Straight tonic with ice, please, George.'

'Comin' up.'

On one of the walls was a huge photo of Emma Watson, at least five foot by five foot. It was not a casual shot, but nor did it look posed. She was leaning slightly to one side, staring directly into the camera with a warm smile, against a backdrop of what looked like Marram grass.

George saw me looking at it. 'Ah yes, Em. She moved in with me, so to speak, when the missus moved out with the kids! ...Or was it the other way round?' He grinned his cheeky cockney grin.

'Is that a pap shot?'

'Nah. When she was little and everyone was 'anging around the 'Arry Potter set, I made an agreement with 'er parents. That if I stayed away from 'er till she was an adult, I would be allowed to take a proper pic, a nice pic. And this is it. Legit!'

'Very nice! You should use it for the article. Headline: "Pervy Pap Goes Straight"!'

George half choked on the swig of lager he had just taken. 'You are a very naughty man, Mr Barry. Very funny. Bit of a comedian. But naughty. Naughty but nice!'

'Talking of "naughty", George, I met a lawyer the other day who worked for the law firm that obtained the super-injunction on behalf of CTF.'

'CTF? ...Ah yes, the name that dare not speak its name... Still got the pic, actually, mate. I told the lawyers I would destroy all copies of it. But. What the 'ell? It's what you might call an... unusual shot! Wanna see it?' I declined. 'Nah. It's pretty grubby. Even for me. But, 'ats off to me, it's a nice piece of work – well composed, sharply focused. And C – what's 'e called again?'

'CTF.'

'Well, yeah, CTF quite recognisably CTF, despite the straining face. From all the shenanigans. Beneath and above. If you see what I mean.'

'But how on earth did you get that photo, George?'

He tapped the side of his nose with his forefinger. 'Al fresco, mate. The garden of delights! I'd been tipped off that the name that dare not speak its name liked the life "oh naturell", so to speak, and was prone… prone. Ha. Geddit? Prone… horizontal, mate – was prone to use his garden for a little bit… or a lottle bit' – he chuckled again – 'of pond-paddling. If yer get me drift. So, me, I stuffed a wadge of notes in a neighbour's 'and and set meself up next door. Mind you, mate, I wasn't exactly expecting the, erm, multi-gender display he provided me with. Quite put me off me dinner!'

He clapped his hands. 'Right! To work! Let's go to my office, mate.'

He led me upstairs to a room filled with the clutter of photography. Lenses, filters, cameras, computer print-outs of photos. A particularly large lens was lying on a camp bed in a corner. 'That's impressive, George,' I said.

'Yeah. 800 millimetres. Weighs nearly five kilos. And cost over ten grand! But it does the job… if the target is a shy little bugger who likes to 'ide away in the distance!'

'What did you start with, George?'

'Canon Sure Shot. When I was a kid. And then I got a Leica M6 with a 50 millimetre lens. Brilliant camera. And all you need is a 50 mil lens to learn the basics of the craft…

Now, mate, how d'yer wanna go about this, eh?'

I told him that I wanted to know something about his childhood, his background. About how he became interested in photography. His early successes.

'Background? I'll tell you what, mate, I think we should invent an interesting backstory for me. Yer know. Exotic like.'

'No, George, I can't do that, I'm afraid. That's not the kind of work I do.'

George guffawed. 'Only kidding, guv! My story is plenty interesting enough.'

'Good! Now. Something I need to establish at the outset is the voice you want to tell the story in. Cockney wide-boy argot? Or idiosyncratic but reasonably polished autodidact?'

'Come again, guv?'

We decided on the latter. He was, after all, trying to move himself upmarket. And he spoke very eloquently about his childhood. His single-parent mum who moved to Reading when he was two. Her desire for him to make the most of his schooling. Her sacrifices to enable him to follow his interests. Photography came very early on. His mother had a bird feeder in their tiny garden and, because she refilled it religiously, it became a regular haunt for garden birds of all kinds. When George told her that he would like to keep a pictorial record of the visitors, she saved up for the Canon Sure Shot and gave it to him one Christmas. He never looked back. And when he left school he went to work in a local camera shop.

'It was great. I learnt so much from the manager and from chatting to customers. But my big break came quite by chance. I was walking along the Thames towpath in Reading with my Leica M6 one day when I came across local girl Kate Winslet walking her dog. It must have been about 1996. She was beginning to make a name for herself. She'd broken through with *Heavenly Creatures* and *Sense and Sensibility*. And things hadn't yet gone completely mental, as they would when *Titanic* came out… She was beautiful. Dressed casually and not particularly made up – just a natural, girl-next-door beauty. I was eighteen, so this was nearly twenty years and four stone ago' – he pats his paunch – 'and I probably looked young and innocent. So when I said, "You're Kate Winslet, aren't you?", she nodded with a gorgeous smile. And, when I asked her if I could take her picture, she nodded again.'

As he was telling me all this, I noticed that George had lost much of his broad cockney accent. Beneath the persona of the irrepressible cockney geezer there seemed to be lurking someone well-spoken and serious-minded.

'I took about six shots. And there was one gorgeous pic that absolutely captured the girl-next-door thing. And I took it to the local paper and they gave me a tenner for it! … And a few days later a photo agency rang me asking to buy the rights. A national paper wanted to use the photo! Well, that was it. I was off. I'd done my garden birds. And now I was moving on to birds of the human feather – birds of paradise!' There was the momentary glint in his eye and the familiar half twitch of his lips that I recognised as a familiar feature of his self-conscious attempts at humour.

He got up from his chair and grabbed my empty glass. 'Ready for a proper one, mate?'

I shook my head. He went downstairs and I heard a hiss-click as George opened another bottle of lager. I paused the voice recorder I had switched on at the beginning of conversation. I was feeling confident that George was giving me the sort of material that I could turn into a decent article for him. When he returned, I asked him what the next big step up had been.

'Well, Kate had made me want to be a celebrity photographer. And funnily enough, I had another chance encounter a few weeks later. I was walking along a track in some meadowland, hoping to find a spot where I might get some interesting bird photographs, when I came across a film crew. And in the midst of the melee was Michael Caine, being led to a car. He got in and was driven to a cottage about four hundred yards down the track. Having a meal, or a break of some kind. The car waited with its driver outside. So I thought I would wait, too. I only had a 50mm lens, so if I wanted a shot I would have to get close. About half an hour later he came out and, as he walked towards the car, he saw me with my camera raised to my face. And here's the amazing thing. In a split second, without breaking stride, he momentarily half turned towards me, with a composed smile on his face. And I got a perfect shot.'

'Which you sold?'

'Nah. No one was interested. Photo agencies were awash with photos of our Michael.'

'So what did you do next?'

'Well, I was aware that the world of professional photographers is very competitive, pretty much a closed shop. That's when I realised I would have to get the shot that nobody else had got. So I asked the manager of the camera shop if I could borrow a super long lens, and eventually he sold me one on the cheap. I carried on working for him for a couple of years, going away at weekends with my long lens. I gradually learnt where to hang out, how to get the saleable shot, who to sell it to. And I built up over the years a notebook with celebrity addresses, phone numbers and car registration plates.'

I wanted to move forward. 'Okay, George, we're going to need some account, in your article, of why you abandoned – note the past tense! – the paparazzi… And we are going to have to create some worthy project for the photojournalist. Now, I've got his idea, especially as your story starts on the Thames with Kate Winslet – a photoshoot of contrasts based on the Thames. Finding some run-down decrepit house-boats that would make interesting pictures, with families who have lived on the river for decades. And contrast them, perhaps, with the huge gin-palace cruisers, with their cargoes of the idle rich at play. So your story starts on the Thames and the narrative arc takes you back there.'

George leapt up from his chair and grabbed me by my arms, squeezing them roughly. 'You are fucking brilliant, Nichol-arse! Fucking brilliant!'

'Thank you… But I'm not sure I like the soubriquet!'

'Come again?'

'The soubriquet. Handle. Soubriquet. Nichol-whatever!'

'Well, never mind the soup-of-the-fucking-day, Nick. You're one cool cookie! I like your idea. Love it! I'm straight on to it, mate.'

*

I had taken the train and tube to get to George's house and decided to take a different route home. I headed towards the river, a short walk away, and hit the towpath just below Chiswick Mall, narrowing at its end to a paved path that separated expensive-looking houses from the river by only a few yards; on the far bank was the Leg o' Mutton, a thriving nature reserve by all accounts.

Enjoying the summer sun sparkling in the water, buoyantly optimistic, I thought of my two newest clients. Carlo, with his exotic pedigree and his banner-waving, culture-changing past, seemed to be a creature in hiding, seeking to camouflage his vibrancy of colour as best he could. George, furtive stalker, hider in ditches and bushes, appeared, by contrast, open and keen to be seen and known. It would be fun, I thought, burrowing into the lives of these two men, teasing away the details until I had the rudiments of a portrait for each, perhaps a cartoonish sketch of George and something more complex for Carlo, something that captured his finer delineations. That was assuming that I would continue with Theresa's projected book on her father. I had not yet made up my mind.

I passed the Civil Service Sports Ground, then a couple of boathouses, and soon was mounting the steps to Barnes Bridge. On my way I had walked past Chiswick Pier, noticing a varied assortment of moored boats; a possible starting point, I thought, for George's project.

*

Back home, I decided to listen to some more of Theresa's tapes of Carlo. He was talking about the launch of *it* – the *International Times* – in October 1966. 'The Poetry Incarnation at the Albert Hall was a massive event. It changed everything. These huge numbers of young people coming together for a poetry event, taking over a staid Victorian building, smoking dope, challenging the establishment with their behaviour and their art, their poetry. I wanted to build on that, keep the momentum going, so I got together some of the people from that event and put the idea to them. At the Albert Hall, there had been a sense of dissidence, of challenge, of wanting to change things... change, yes, change the whole world. And we thought we could do it—'

Theresa interrupts. 'Really, Papa? Young people really thought that, that they could change things?'

'They did. We did. We had created our own music, our own culture, our own politics, our own morality. And all these things were different from our parents' generation. Rock music, Beat poetry, radical politics, free love—'

'All the things we've got now. Or most of.'

'Exactly. We fought for them and won these freedoms for you.'

Theresa makes an indeterminate noise. I couldn't tell whether she was expressing approval or scepticism. It didn't strike me that young people today felt particularly free, so I assumed it was the latter. But hearing that noise reminded me of that brief folly of love-making. And for a moment, I was longing to see her again.

'So, tell me about the magazine. *it.*'

'Well, we set up in small offices in Southampton Row. And we got a variety of people – poets, political activists – to write for us. We wanted to mix it all up – to have a mix of fashion, music, literature, drugs, sex, radical politics. We wanted to cross-pollinate all these different groups. We hoped it would be a truly international cultural interchange. I know you find this hard to believe, Tease, but we really did think we could change the world… And we had this great launch at the Roundhouse. The building was pretty much a wreck. Hadn't been used for trains for decades. I think it had become a bonded warehouse for booze, or something. I'm sure it was a complete firetrap at the time. Anyway, the playwright and activist, Arnold Wesker, he had bought a lease on it, hoping to turn it into an arts centre. So I rang him up and asked if we could use it for our launch party. And John Hopkins – a big man in the sixties, you've probably not heard of him – he got Pink Floyd – you have heard of them, I'm sure – to play for us. And the evening was the Albert Hall all over again. An assertion of the Alternative Society. Two fingers to the establishment. And sex, drugs, and rock and roll. Lots of it!'

Theresa laughs. And then she asks, 'Why was it called *it*?'

'I wanted to capture the sense of the moment. The essence of something. The it-ness. When someone asked what "IT" stood for I immediately said, without thinking, "International Times". And that was perfect, suggesting our intended outreach.'

'And what kind of things were you writing about?'

'Things we wanted to change. Such as stopping the Vietnam War, opposing apartheid in South Africa… scrapping pub-licensing laws, making London an all-night city, with tubes running twenty-four hours a day. And advice. On squatting in unoccupied houses, on drugs, sex and those kinds of things.'

'How long did it run for, Papa?'

'It was a great success in the early days. But to be honest, it wasn't very well run. Once I had set it up, I moved on to other things. But the people who ran it were hopeless at admin. At getting stuff written for it on a regular basis, at distribution, at getting money in for it. It stumbled on into the '70s, but it had had its day.'

I switched off the tape. Carlo's recollections were undeniably interesting. To have been there at the heart of so much; that would make an interesting story, for sure. And that strange noise that Theresa had made on the tape. That made me want to see her again.

So I rang her that evening to discuss the next stage of the project.

7

I had ordered two books about the 1960s that Vikki had suggested might be useful for my research on Carlo. One was a hefty tome written ten years earlier, 950 pages of close socio-politico-cultural analysis, which would offer a wealth of background material for researching the detail and textures of the decade. The other was an older book, published in the 1980s; it was a lengthy anthology of interviews with some of the more important movers and shakers of the sixties.

I thought I would start with the latter. It looked like it would give me a good sense of the mood, the atmosphere, perhaps even the voice of the sixties – and I flipped through it superficially over breakfast. Great care had clearly been taken over the composition of the book. Rather than being organised into chapters, there were hundreds of section-headers, whimsically worded and often containing a nugatory quotation, each with several hundred- to two hundred-word contributions on the topic, headings such as 'Tripping Out: "If you stand on tippytoe you can touch the ceiling"'. At the back there were brief biographies of all the contributors. It was going to be a useful document in giving me a feel for the elusive decade.

But here was the strange thing. Carlo d'Abruzzi had not been deemed by the editor of this book to be important enough to be a contributor. Stranger still, he did not even appear in the index. Even more worrying was my discovery that he was not in the index of the other book either, the 950-pager.

When I had spoken to Theresa the night before, it had been to arrange to meet Carlo on neutral ground. I had explained to her why I often did this in the early stages of a project. 'I have found from experience, Theresa, that home, or somewhere familiar, but especially home, often exerts a kind of magnetic field force that can distort... distort memories, impressions, all kinds of things. Being in a neutral environment tends to focus the mind, to minimise the distortions... Do you think it would be possible to see you father away from his home?'

'I'm sure it would,' she said. It was so nice to be hearing her voice after my self-imposed exile. 'He's got to come up London in the next fortnight to get a new pair of shoes – don't ask! – and he doesn't really like sleeping here. So I could book him into a hotel he quite likes in Brook Green. I could book you both in, if you like.'

And that's what we agreed. That he would travel up the following Tuesday in the morning. Have a session with me in the afternoon, and possibly into the evening. Buy his shoes in town the following morning and then travel back down to Dorset.

Of course, my whole job had been made that much harder by the discovery that Carlo appeared to be an invisible force in the sixties, absent from the indexes of two important works about the decade.

*

Being a freelance writer offers little security. The work that brings in regular pay-cheques – ghosting newspaper columns for celebrities, footballers, or politicians or whoever – rarely pays well. So it is the big projects – the autobiographies, in particular – that one is seeking. I'd still not come to any arrangement on the kind of fee I would get for the Carlo book. Vikki needed to see my synopsis before that could be moved forward. George Nelson would no doubt be generous if I came up with an article that he was pleased with and which he could place. The fact was, however, that I was always looking for new avenues, to ensure that the money kept coming in, that my future security was assured.

Today I was heading to London to meet a twenty-six-year-old soap star. I was on her (more likely her agent's) short-list of potential freelancers to ghost her autobiography. I have always thought that the notion of anybody under the age of forty, even fifty, writing an autobiography is more than mildly ridiculous. More auto than bio, in the sense of these things invariably being self-interested grabs at the quick buck rather than examinations of lives of substance. More auto than bio and, of course, because the -graphy part of it tends to be beyond the wit of the young celebrity, the task of actually writing up the slender pickings of a young life will normally fall to the likes of me.

I am not being entirely fair. There are books that have been written about young lives that, while being occasioned by brief or not-so-brief moments of celebrity, have had their real interest in the backgrounds of the people rather than their fame and achievement; the real achievement being their struggle against some kind of adversity, their triumph over hostile circumstances. Certainly I have written some accounts where the glitz of a young life has covered an aching childhood that the subject has struggled out of with impressive determination.

Travelling up to Waterloo, I recalled the projected autobiography of a forty-something actor I had been commissioned to ghost a few years earlier. I had done lots of homework and was confident that there was a good book in the offing. The man had started his career as the lead in a long-running television drama series in the 1980s. Worried that he might become typecast if he stayed for too long in the role, he had courageously jumped ship at the height of his success. But he was a good actor and he found a number of film roles in the following years and plenty of television work. And then, in his late thirties he was offered the lead role in a new flagship television series and quickly became a darling of the tele-viewing nation. Hence the call for an autobiography.

He was an entirely likeable man: intelligent, unassuming, articulate. And our early meetings were productive and enjoyable. I learnt about his childhood – no great revelations there, but interesting nonetheless – his years at drama school, and the excitement every time he landed and explored a significant new role.

But one day, when we met, he turned up sheepishly and delivered a bombshell. He was abandoning the project. It was empty, worthless. I still remember the very words he used. 'I've realised, through my conversations with you, that my achievements are negligible, meaningless. I am a fraud.' That's what he said: 'I am a fraud.' And he said he didn't want to proceed with the autobiography. That he would reimburse me for the time I had spent on him. That he would pay back the publisher's advance.

There was a hint of sadness in his face. But he didn't seem depressed. Just very matter-of-fact. He said something like, 'I've come to realise that I'm hollow, that I don't have any real personality at all. Maybe that is why I became an actor, to inhabit characters of real substance, to play at being someone. But when I take off the mask at the end of the day, there is nothing, or very little. Someone very ordinary and uninteresting. That's why I don't think I should be writing an autobiography. It would be a con, a fraud.'

I told him that people would like to hear about the roles he'd played, the scrapes he had got into on the film or television set, the people he had worked with. His readers would be interested in his anecdotes about other famous actors. But he was adamant. No autobiography. No empty stories about other celebrities, many of whom, he said, were probably just as ordinary and uninteresting in their real lives as him. 'Celebrity,' I remember him saying, 'is a mask, sometimes elaborately constructed. But I can't tell you what a relief it is for me to take it off each night when I get home and am with my family.'

*

My celebrity today was taking time out from Walford and she had, rather incongruously and somewhat ostentatiously, booked a room in the Dorchester hotel to conduct her interviews. The suite was at the cheaper end of what this extravagantly indulgent hotel had to offer, but stylish enough, with its spaciousness and its tasteful art deco ambience. I am going to call her Tracey Fry. This, of course, is not her real name. However, those of you well-versed in such television drama, especially that coming out of Walford, might well be able to guess her identity. She was currently a focus of attention in the tabloids. She had split with her celebrity partner and there was speculation that he, or someone else, had left her pregnant. This, of course, was absolutely none of my concern today.

The agent was a middle-aged woman. Large, child-like blue eyes dominated a face that had once been very beautiful, I suspected, but now was blurring and coarsening with age. She spoke with a diction that smacked of trained elocution. I suspected she was an actress who had never quite made the grade; or perhaps someone who simply felt she could make a better living out of managing the careers of other actors rather than maintaining her own.

She introduced me to the soap star, directed me to a chair, and got the meeting underway. 'Right, Nick, you are one of five people we are considering to help Tracey with her autobiography.' She tilted her head forward a little and peered over her glasses, adding, 'The only man, I might say… So, Tracey is going to talk about the kind of book she wants. She will tell you about the kinds of things she wants to focus upon. And we'll follow this with a discussion, and perhaps a Q&A.'

I nodded, and waited for Tracey to begin. Tracey, our East End girl in a posh West End hotel. She was presentably dressed in tight-fitting designer jeans and a printed blouse that looked very expensive. She was smaller than she appeared on television and, although she was quite heavily made up, her skin looked less youthful, had less of a bloom than that of her TV character; the beginnings, perhaps, of those ravages that actors' makeup sometimes inflicts on sensitive skins. Her lips were a self-inflicted ravage. They had been fashionably over-plumped, giving her a somewhat grotesque piscine pout.

'So.' The voice was a surprise. There was a less pronounced cockney accent than her character's, but what the actress had and the character didn't – as far as I remembered – was a pronounced vocal fry. The vowel of 'so' was stretched out unnaturally, dipping to a scratchy conclusion. 'I want to revisit my childhood. My mum struggling to bring me up after my violent father walked out. Scrimping and saving and moving heaven and earth to get me into a performing arts school.'

Her vocal chords were flapping away as they tightened and slackened irregularly, the breath bubbling and popping and rattling in a low, masculine frequency. When I was at school I could not bear the sound of a teacher's fingernail catching on the blackboard, emitting that horrendous high-pitched screech; it went right through my body. The vocal fry catches a nerve in the same way. I can't bear the sound. And I can't understand why this vocal tick of such unremitting ugliness, imitative of young American celebrity women, has caught on in this country. Tracey sounded like she had the death rattle. I wanted to be out of that room as quickly as possible.

But I had to endure. I was making sketchy notes as she continued. 'And I want to write about the stuff I watched

on telly when I was little, the actors I wanted to be like.'
I nodded. 'And going for my first audition and getting a
small part as a teenage girl in *Casualty*.' The first syllable
of "Casualty" was airborne for a split second, and then
'teeeeeee' came slowly crashing down with a long, rasping
series of croaks.

By the time she had finished, prompted at times by both
her agent and me, I had a pretty good idea of what she was
expecting. Apart from the obvious biographical detail, she
clearly wanted the first part of the book to be a tribute to
her mother and pay-back time for her father. She wanted
the Walford years to be a showcase for the wonderfully
talented and professional actress she considered herself to
be; and a veritable gossip column about her fellow actors in
the soap: the lovely people, the bitches, the bastards.

The agent was aware of my track record with
autobiographies and presumably thought I was up to
scratch, otherwise I would not have been on the short-list
of possible ghosts. I suspected that the real purpose of the
meeting was to see how I got on with Tracey; to observe the
vibe between us. When she felt she had seen enough, she
said we were done. She would be in touch in due course.

As I walked out of the hotel into Park Lane, I thought
how refreshingly pleasant the London traffic sounded after
the prolonged abrasive assault of Tracey's vocal chords. I
was absolutely sure that the agent would have noticed the
complete absence of any warmth between Tracey and me.
And I knew that there was zero chance of my being offered
the commission. For which I was very glad.

Suddenly, out of the corner of my eye, as I was heading
towards the tube station, I caught sight of George Nelson.

He was half hidden by a plane tree on the grassy central reservation that separated the two carriageways of Park Lane. I drew two fingers to my eyes, pointed a single finger towards him and then tapped my nose. 'I can see you, you old rogue,' I muttered, half under my breath. He grinned and hoisted his camera in the air to indicate what he was up to. As if I didn't know. I hadn't told him I was seeing Tracey Fry, still less where, but he perhaps had followed her to the hotel. And now he would wait until he got what he deemed to be the money shot as she exited. No doubt he was hoping that his powerful lens would bring confirmation of Tracey's growing bump.

*

There was a message on my landline phone when I got home. It was Vikki reminding me that I had still not sent the chapter synopsis of the proposed book on Carlo. I would rather have waited until after my meeting with him up in town the following week but decided I would put something together. I could always amend it if necessary if Carlo made some new and startling revelations.

When Theresa had made her recordings of her father, she had helpfully produced some kind of index on the sleeves of the cassette boxes. So I looked at these, made a note of subjects that might usefully provide chapter topics, and set to work. I had not listened to all the tapes, so there were items in the index and in my outline which I was taking a chance on. I had fun making up the titles and subtitles. If Vikki thought they were too jokey, or just plain silly, I could always change them. So this was the synopsis I emailed off her:

The Boat Comes In
*D'Abruzzi's discovery of the Beatles; his
meetings with Epstein*

Hey, Mister Grey Sky
1950s Britain; d'Abruzzi's early life

The Beats Go On
*The International Poetry Incarnation at the
Albert Hall; youth culture*

The Geometry of Fashion
Mary Quant; Biba

Opening the Doors
*Promoting The Doors' concert at the
Roundhouse; the drug culture*

Taking the Underground
Political activism; rebellion

Zen Bones
Religion; mysticism

Coasting
*D'Abruzzi abandons London and heads for a
teaching job on the south coast*

8

I had arranged to meet Theresa and Carlo for lunch at the Café Rouge restaurant on Shepherd's Bush Road. They were looking at menus when I arrived and both stood up to welcome me, Theresa giving me a light peck on the cheek and Carlo warmly shaking my hand. 'Good to see you again, Nick.' I was surprised at how positively and enthusiastically he greeted me. His eyes were lively, friendly, with none of the suspicion I had seen in them on that first meeting down in Dorset. He was dressed for the country rather than the city: light twill trousers, check shirt, cravat and tweed jacket; and he looked fit and healthy.

'Papa has brought you a little present, Nick!' Theresa said as, from a carrier bag, Carlo withdrew a ledger of some sort, handing it to me, his face cracking into a boyish smile. 'It's notes from his early days of lecturing and of designing the Cultural Studies course!' Theresa was spilling excitement as she spoke, thrilled at how positive her father was being, at the sweetness of nature he was showing to me. I wondered whether she had worked on him, briefed him, perhaps even suggesting the present, to ensure that all went well.

There was something about the café that seemed to animate Carlo. The vibrant colours, perhaps, or the slightly retro feel to it. Or perhaps it was simply being out and about amidst the busyness and noise of London. It was a delight to see him, perched on a red banquette, sparkling away, chattering to Theresa, smiling warmly at me every now and again, and looking with interest every time somebody new came into the café. And I could swear I had seen him cast mildly libidinous glances at a young waitress as she moved back and forth between the tables.

After lunch Theresa took us to our hotel, a short walk down the road, which was filled with a slow and noisy procession of cars and lorries and buses.

'Papa always has a quick nap after lunch,' she said. 'But after that he is all yours until supper. I've booked an early meal for the two of you here in the hotel. Papa will want an early night, I'm sure, won't you, Papa?'

He nodded. And then, with a farewell kiss on her father's cheek, she left us.

*

At about half-past two there was a knock on my door. Carlo's eyes had less of a twinkle than at lunch time, perhaps because he was still a little bleary from his nap. Or perhaps the old nervousness with me, the suspicion, had resurfaced. The next few hours would tell me which. In fact, I was certain that the next few hours would give me my final answer as to whether the Carlo commission was a runner or not.

Before coming to Hammersmith, I had worked my way through all the tapes of Theresa's interviews with her father and had made notes of the areas I wanted to talk about. And at the beginning of the previous week I had sent him the completed draft of the first chapter of the proposed book, so that he might get a feel of the way I was going to write about his life. It seemed a good way into conversation this afternoon, so I started by asking him what he'd thought about it.

'Yes, very good. You write well. And I liked the way you framed the chapter with the two meetings with Epstein. Not so sure about the prince bit, though.' There was a half chuckle as he said this, perhaps more of a dismissive snort, and his eyes had that momentary opacity that I remembered from my visit to Dorset.

'Well, I think it works. It creates a sense of the exotic, which will fit in well with the main narrative line: the lifting, in the 1960s, of the grey veil of the post-war years and the explosion into the vivid technicolour dream of the sixties.'

He grinned – the uninhibited, warming smile that Theresa had inherited from him. 'Yes, I suppose you're right.'

I asked if he was happy with the third-person narrative, telling him that Theresa had thought that the story should be in the first person, in his voice.

'Oh no, that would be much too complicated.'

'Not at all. That's what I do much of the time – tell the stories of others in their own voices.'

He said he would think about it.

I reminded him that the opening chapter ended with him heading to the Roundhouse in the hope of arranging an all-night concert with The Doors and Jefferson Airplane.

'Ah yes, that was quite an event. I remember it all so clearly. Visually it was all very low-key compared with the kind of rock concerts that came later. Simple rostrum stage, dull drapes behind. No seating to speak of, just the floor in what was a barn of a building. Jefferson Airplane had brought a lightshow with them – state-of-the-art at the time, I guess, but very unsophisticated by today's standards. Jim Morrison, of course, was really what people had come to see. And he didn't disappoint. Black leathers and with this huge head of hair. Moody, aggressive. A kind of James Dean untameability. Like the Poetry bash as the Albert Hall in '65 and the launch of *it* in '66, it was momentous event. Truly memorable.'

'So were you part of Middle Earth?' I asked. I wasn't trying to wrong-foot Carlo, but he seemed startled.

'What?'

'I've seen copies of the posters advertising the concert. It seems to have been promoted by Middle Earth.'

'Oh.' The evasive look. '…Ah. Well, yes, I guess that was the vehicle I used to get the thing off the ground. If I remember rightly I used a middleman. Guess he could have called himself Middle Earth… Figures.'

We then talked about the drugs culture of the time. I explained to him how the section of the book on The Doors concert would broaden into an account of the drugs scene: the new substances available; the ease of getting hold of them; the acceptance by the young.

'Well, yes,' he said, 'a good link – The Doors of Perception. Huxley and Timothy Leary. The thing is, Nick, that drugs have since become recreational at best and deeply destructive at worst. But in the sixties, they were seen as a kind of sacramental pathway to a higher consciousness. They offered a way of finding your true self. "Come sweetly back to myself as I was". The true self. The forgotten self. Do you recognise that line? "Come sweetly back to myself as I was"?' I shook my head. 'Ginsberg. Truly great man.'

'You say that drugs were regarded as a kind of "sacramental pathway". Did you do a lot of drugs, Carlo?'

'Well, a fair amount. Cannabis, of course. Coke occasionally. And quite a lot of acid.'

'And was it consciousness-expanding?'

'Well, here's the strange thing, Nick. It absolutely changed the way I saw things. I must have been naïve before, but you see I had this incredible acid trip one time. I was in a friend's back garden, quite an ordinary garden, there were three or four of us. I remember spending what seemed like hours staring at the clouds, gazing up in wonder, observing the slowly dissolving patterns and reassembling shapes and being in awe of it all. But the real mind-opening experience came from looking at this ordinary garden. Very ordinary, with an uncared-for lawn and a meagre border of plants running along the stone boundary wall. But all of it, all of it, the grass, the flowers, the stones in the wall, they all looked... they all had the appearance and texture of the thick brush-strokes of a van Gogh painting. And it was a real insight to me – naïve as I must have been. I suddenly realised that the paintings of people like van Gogh were not consciously stylised. These people were painting what they saw! It changed the whole way I understood the nature of perception.'

It was the first time I had ever heard real energy and real enthusiasm in Carlo's voice. For a moment I imagined

Carlo, the worshipped father, telling his excited daughter the tales of his youth. And for a moment the image – not of father and daughter, of course – of Desdemona's greedy ear being ravished by the wondrous tales of Othello came to mind; and I pictured the young Theresa pestering her father for more stories and listening with excited admiration to his great exploits and achievements.

I was still not ready to mention to Carlo my discovery that he seemed to have been overlooked in two major works about the sixties. I was sure that it would kill the positive atmosphere in an instant. But I did want to hear more about his background: his ancestry and his childhood, which my agent had said I should include at some stage in the story.

I suggested he tell me a little more about his parents, explaining that my agent wanted a section in the book on his ancestry. Immediately the guarded look shadowed his face once more. It was not an aggressive expression, nor even the suspicious look that I had become familiar with. But there seemed to be something troubling him.

'It's just,' I said, 'that when Theresa asked you, on the tapes, why she never saw any relatives, any uncles or aunts, you seemed to get very upset.' There was a very long pause, his face pained. Suddenly this small little room, so unlike the Dorchester suite in which I had met Tracey Fry a few days earlier, became oppressive. I worried that I had asked the wrong question, the question that would bring everything, the whole venture, crashing down.

But he seemed intent on staying the course, on answering anything I asked him. I was sure, now, that Theresa had given him a talking-to, explaining to him the importance of remaining as open with me as possible. 'Yes,

I was upset, of course. I'd lost my parents, fled the country of my birth… Of course I found it upsetting when Theresa asked me about it.'

'Naturally,' I said. 'But presumably there were relatives who were still alive. Cousins, uncles, aunts, great-uncles, great-aunts—'

'Of course… But… but my parents' marriage had split the families. I never knew any grandparents, any uncles or aunts when I was little, and then I was gone to England.'

'Tell me about your parents.' I was interested in going further than the information I had learnt from the tapes and from my earlier discussion with him.

'My father was called Victor; he was the son of Prince Umberto, Count of Salemi, who was the grandson of Victor Emmanuel II, King of Italy. His maternal grandmother, Maria Letizia Bonaparte, was a great niece of Napoleon.' The sing-song voice returned, the sense of a ritual, of a memory being intoned. I remembered how unsettling I'd found it when I had visited him in Dorset. Victor was new. As far as I remembered it from that earlier occasion, he had said that Umberto was his father.

'And your mother?'

He struggled with his answer. It looked for a moment as though he was scouring his memory, digging deep for her name; and then I realised that the struggle was with pain, the pain of loss. 'My mother,' he said, '…my mother was called Rosa. She was a beautiful woman by all accounts… But she was not of great birth, an ordinary woman of humble stock—'

'Which would explain the estrangement between the two families.'

'What? ...Um... Yes, of course.'

The mood of our meeting had changed and, although I could have questioned him on the name of his mother – in Theresa's interview he had called her Maria rather than Rosa – I was worried that I was wasting the opportunity to explore other, less painful parts of Carlo's life. So I asked him about his move to the south coast, about upping sticks and turning his back on the pulsating London scene. He looked at me intently, with a slight air of puzzlement, I'm not sure why, perhaps trying to assess whether I really was interested in this part of his life.

So I prompted him. 'I think you said on tape that you had taken the movement as far as possible.'

Another pause. 'Well, yes, movements are interesting, both in terms of groups of people coming together with shared ideals and in terms of historical directions... We like to divide things up into decades and make silly... simple assumptions about these random divisions of time, slapping labels on them, simplifying them. The grey fifties, the swinging sixties, the loadsa-money culture of the eighties. But history is not like that at all... I suppose that it was really when I began to think about these things – movements, trends, fashions, and the things that moulded all these forces – that I became interested in Cultural Studies.'

He talked for some time about the way cultural forces are fashioned, randomly to a certain extent, driven by industrial and technological inventions, by changes of the political climate. He spoke with the same warmth, the same animation that he had spoken with when describing the epiphany into perception he had received during that notable LSD trip, the rheumy eyes alive and glistening.

At some stage we had a break for tea. We spoke of all kinds of things that afternoon and there was often excitement in his voice as he described some of the great experiences in his life, especially in the 1960s. But as evening approached, with supper time not far off, a gloom seemed to descend upon him. Perhaps I had simply tired him out. He was an old man, an old man living in the penumbra of dementia, according to Theresa, though there had been little evidence of it in our conversation.

Until... until he said by way of nothing, 'You know, Nick, you must forgive me my memory. It's slowly going and I'll slipping into forgetful ignorance—'

'Absolutely not!' I said. 'You've been sharp as a nail with your memories this afternoon.'

He laughed gently. 'That's kind. But things do jumble up. Sometimes I have to invent to cover my forgetfulness or my ignorance... And I get these momentary lapses sometimes when I seem to forget who I am.'

'Carlo d'Abruzzi! The working title of my book is *Catalysing the Counter Culture*. So you are Carlo d'Abruzzi, catalyst of the counter-culture.' He had been in such good spirits that I thought this might make him laugh, or at least smile with a grateful acknowledgement of the importance I was attaching to him. But instead, he looked agonised, with a hint of panic, too, perhaps, eyes darting.

He brought the subject back to his lecturing, to his happy life in Dorset, to the wonderful sense of blessing he felt when he and his wife Brenda were gifted, late in his life, with Theresa and Luca.

How had he come to meet Brenda, I wondered.

'She worked at the Institute. In the library. I wasn't

particularly looking for a wife, looking for love even, but we used to chat sometimes and there was some kind of spark there. So I plucked up the courage and asked her out! And it slowly grew from there… She was a wonderful wife. And a wonderful mother.' The seeming panic of a moment ago was gone, the darting eyes stilled into a warm, relaxed smile.

'Tragic that she should die so young.'

The smile vanished in an instant. He paused and swallowed and said in a hoarse voice, 'And I was alone again… Except I had the children, young, young children… And the one thing I knew was that I had to be there for them.'

At supper we talked of other things, trivial mostly. Before we finished our meal we were joined by Theresa.

'How are the boys?' she asked.

'The boys have had a great afternoon,' I replied. 'Very productive.'

She looked at her father, seeking confirmation. He nodded. And, as he looked at her, there was a smile of pride on his face, a little-boy smile of pride, acknowledgement of a task carried out obediently and successfully.

*

When Carlo went for his early night, I went to my room, too, to check that my voice recorder had picked up our conversation clearly, and to make notes of my immediate impressions. At about ten o'clock Theresa rang to say that she was in the hotel bar; would I join her for a nightcap?

She was thrilled with the positive frame of mind that she had found her father in when she had joined us earlier in the evening. 'He looked so relaxed. So happy!'

'Yes,' I agreed. 'He was in very good form. There were one or two areas that I steered clear of… that I didn't feel confident of raising with him—'

'Such as?'

'Well… Well, I would like to have asked him why he doesn't appear in either of two important books about the sixties that one might expect him to appear in. But it's not important at this stage.'

Theresa's excitement, her sense of achievement at having engineered such a productive afternoon for me, was such that nothing would be allowed to sour the day for her. 'I don't think that's an issue really, Nick. As I think I have told you before, he sometimes used other names. Charlie Adams, for example… I mean, you can understand it. He might have felt that parading himself as Prince Carlo d'Abruzzi was not entirely appropriate to an anti-establishment movement.' She laughed. 'I mean, you can see it, can't you?'

I nodded. I loved her enthusiasm. I loved the girlish excitement; it was a torrent that swept all obstacles aside, the power of its momentum carrying everything forward to the great conclusion she anticipated: my celebration of her father's life.

We talked some more and then, when I said it was time to hit the sack, she asked in an unsettlingly child-like voice, 'Is there room for a little one?'

I had assumed that we both regarded our carnal moment on the night of her dinner party as a one-off. 'Is that wise, do you think?'

'I don't see why not. And you're due another bonus, I reckon!' She laughed some more, her eyes sparkling mischief, and she reached a hand out to mine.

Despite an instant stirring in me, I considered declining her offer; doing the sensible thing. But I quickly decided that it would probably be more complicated to reject her invitation than comply with it. I saw that she clearly regarded bedding me as a transaction of some sort, without any consequences or complications. Besides, the instant stirring was turning into something more urgent, with an increasing sense of compulsion.

So we went up to my room and got undressed. We took each other with no less appetite than on our first coupling, and in my case – unlike that first time – with no post-coital regret. When we had finished, and lain silently in bed together for a while, she got up, went to the bathroom, got dressed and left, saying she would see me for breakfast the following morning. Business-like, without complication.

*

After breakfast, we decided that we would all three walk to Hammersmith tube station together, Carlo and Theresa to head up to town to buy some shoes, me to make my way home for a day of writing.

The roads were, as ever in London, busy and noisy. On the pavements people hurried to work or to shop, jostling as they went. Carlo had lost some of the previous day's positivity. At breakfast he had seemed a little distrait.

But, nothing, absolutely nothing, could have prepared us for what was about to happen next. Theresa had just pointed out a restaurant to me, saying that we should eat there when I was next in the area – it had built up a fine reputation in recent years. The moments which followed have been seared into my brain. When the video chooses to replay itself – and I have very little control of when this might be – it is unvarying in its sequence of events and in its detail.

Unnoticed by either Theresa or me, Carlo has absent-mindedly drifted out into the road. Before either of us can shout to him, he is over halfway across. At that moment a single-decker bus swings rather too quickly around the corner. Carlo sees it too late. He tries to quicken his pace; and instinctively and futilely his arm rises to fend off the oncoming vehicle. He is knocked off his feet, his torso arcing downwards so that for a moment his body is horizontally parallel with the road, suspended for a split second before falling to the tarmac under the front offside wheel of the bus.

The bus halts. There is no sign of Carlo. As Theresa and I run from the pavement the driver scrambles out of the passenger door. All three of us are halted in our tracks as though running into a hard, invisible wall. Shocked to momentary stillness. The lower half of Carlo's body, his legs at impossible angles, is protruding; the darkening circle of an emptied bladder is expanding around the crotch of his trousers. But the torso is invisible; and it can only – the chest, the neck, perhaps – have gone under the wheel of the bus. Theresa covers her face with her hands. A brief wobble and the driver falls to the ground in a faint.

There is, of course, a soundtrack to this video, too. I am never sure if it is properly or fully synced with the visual images. It starts with a shriek from Theresa that stretches into a prolonged scream and then becomes a steady wail. Almost simultaneous with the shriek is a ridiculously loud bang as the body meets the metal of the bus, followed immediately by a dull crunch of the wheel making contact with the torso of Carlo. For a moment the only noise is coming from Theresa, and then there is a gentle thud as the driver hits the ground. Gradually mutters of shock and disbelief and dismay mount from bystanders, witnesses to this ghastly scene, and become a dissonant blur of noise.

9

Upheaval

A little boy is saying goodbye to his mother before his nanny takes him off to nursery. He is hugging her, his head pressed to her stomach, his hands joining where the small of her back swells into the curve of her hips. Around his head are his mother's hands; they are affectionately tousling and then smoothing his hair.

They are in the small kitchen of their apartment. On the breakfast table the crockery has not yet been cleared. A half-eaten piece of toast remains on the little boy's plate, his favourite plate, one of a set of Limoges's Louis Lourioux Le Faune collection. At the centre of the gold-rimmed dish is a nuthatch. The boy loves the colours of this creature, less gaudy than some of the other birds that adorn the dinner set; and he loves the sleek shape and the long, sharp beak.

'Be a good boy, Carlo,' his mother says, bending down to kiss the top of his head. 'Be good. Enjoy yourself. And I'll see you this afternoon.'

That afternoon there will unexpectedly be a change in routine. It is not the nanny who comes to pick up Carlo. Instead it is the boy's father, who is looking very solemn. He is solemn because he has some dreadful news. During the morning Carlo's mother has unexpectedly died, has shockingly, without warning, taken her leave of her family. The boy's face crinkles. Tears explode from his eyes, splintering his view of his distressed father. The image of that final scene in the kitchen with his mother will never leave him and nor will the tear-fractured image of his unhappy father.

Another image, a happier image, which will remain with the little boy is the memory of a sunlit day of blue; blue sky and the blue, blue sea of the Adriatic. Of turning about and seeing the sparkling rays of sunshine irradiating the grand municipal buildings of the Piazza Unità d'Italia, those monuments to an imperial age, mellowed by the glare of sunlight. In his memory, the little boy, Carlo, is holding the hand of his nanny, who is telling him that he is a little prince, telling him about his father's royal lineage, about his great-grandfather, King Victor Emmanuel II of Italy.

Later, it will be the nanny who will come to this sad little boy, still grieving the death of his mother, and whisk him away from the apartment for the last time. Carlo's father has been killed in an air crash. It is 1940. It is time to go to England, to visit some friends, says the nanny, to seek help from them, to find refuge and peace for a little boy whose life has been torn apart by war and by the sudden deaths of his parents.

*

A sad, frightened little boy awakes to his first English dawn. He hardly dares get out of bed, his own bed at last, after a succession of beds and sofas and floors on his long journey across Europe. There have been moments when he has been confused, moments when he has been scared. But always, always at his side has been his nanny, who has kept his spirits up, told him he will soon be there, cheered him up with silly jokes whenever his face has crumpled.

And now she is with him in his new bedroom, sitting on the edge of his bed, telling him that there is some breakfast for him downstairs. 'But first,' she says, 'you must look out of the window. See where we are!' It had been dark when they had arrived the night before. Exhausted, he had been taken straight upstairs and put to bed. 'You are going to like it here, Carlo, I know you are!'

Carlo goes to the window and looks out. Lush farmland. In a large field stretching up a gentle hill are sheep. In another, closer to the farmhouse, are some cattle.

'This is your new home, Carlo!'

He tries to smile. But it is all too much for him. The journey. The new surroundings. And the dreaded ordeal of meeting Dora and Leonard, the foster parents that his nanny has been telling him about as they have crossed Europe.

'Be brave, Carlo. They are lovely people.'

And she takes him down. Dora looks joyful to see the little boy. She holds out her arms in a welcome and his nanny pushes Carlo towards her. He is timid, uncomfortable, so Dora does not force herself upon him. She asks him if he would like some breakfast.

He nods shyly.

And then Leonard says that after breakfast he will show Carlo the farm, the cows, the sheep, the barns. He speaks slowly and simply, with much gesturing. He is aware that Carlo has little English. What little he has his nanny has taught him as they have journeyed towards England.

It is here, at Barton Farm in west Devon, that Carlo's new life will begin. But not with his nanny. She will not be staying.

By the end of the day she is gone. More loss. More pain.

*

I wrote this piece for my book on Carlo d'Abruzzi on the day that he died. I wrote it when I got home after the great trauma, wrote it to distract myself, to sweeten my mind. I came home overwhelmed with shock; with a kind of grief. Strange, I thought, because I had only met the man twice. I suppose I was suffering vicariously for Theresa. My heart ached for her.

In the moments after the accident, a taxi driver had leapt from his cab and stopped the traffic behind him. A young woman had rushed towards Theresa to drag her away from the terrible scene. And a café manager, who had seen the unfolding horror, had come to us and invited us into his café, seating Theresa down with her back to the road.

Outside I could see people on their phones – calling the emergency services, no doubt – and soon the air was filled with the sound of sirens. Some people were gawping at the scene in a grotesque way and taking photos on their phones, ghouls who would momentarily satisfy their morbid curiosity only until the police shooed them off. Young mothers who were just arriving, unaware of what had happened, gasped and hurried their children quickly away.

Slowly, their arrival delayed by the sclerotic blockage of surrounding roads, emergency vehicles appeared: a fire engine, several police cars, three ambulances, a pick-up truck to lift the front of the bus. All there to deal with the remains of the man who, as a little boy, had left war-torn Trieste for refuge in England. A screen had been erected around the front of the bus so that the grisly task of recovering the body could not be witnessed.

Theresa saw none of this. She was slumped over a table, back to the road, her head in her hands, her body heaving with the spasms of a bottomless grief. The kind café manager had offered her a choice of reviving drinks – tea or coffee, or something stronger if she would like. But she was gone, had retreated into a world beyond any communication. The manager had also turned around the sign on the door so that newcomers would see that the café was now closed. Those finishing off their coffees and side plates were talking quietly, stealing quick and sympathetic glances towards Theresa; they dared not catch her eye, which in any case was unlikely.

A paramedic had come into the café and was talking to her. He could get little from her; her continued sobbing made speech impossible, even if she had been inclined. The paramedic asked me Theresa's name.

'Theresa, I'm Steve, and I'm here to help you… in your own time, Theresa. We're here to help.'

A policeman came in and took my details. And I suddenly realised that Luca did not know what had happened. I asked the café manager if there was a quiet place from which I could make a phone call; he led me to a small rest room behind the kitchen.

I had never had to break bad news before, but I suspected that attempts at softening the blow merely make the final shock the greater; like delaying a dramatic climax for maximum effect. So I told him bluntly. 'Luca, I've got some terrible news, I'm afraid. Your father has been killed in a road accident.'

He was, of course, stunned, but quickly regained his composure and said he would join us in Hammersmith as soon as he could.

When he arrived he took Theresa in his arms. He caught her limp and passive body in a tight embrace, and soon his shoulders were shaking. As he recovered himself he took control, urging me to go: he could take care of things from now on. So I did, telling the policeman I was heading home.

*

Writing the account of the young Carlo, rooted in the facts that he and Theresa had given me, but expanded imaginatively, had made me very sad. But I needed to continue writing. I needed the distraction. So I decided to write the first part of George Nelson's story. I wanted to write the beginning of it so I could run it past him to see if he approved of the voice I'd given him. Of course, as far as I knew, he hadn't undertaken the photoshoot along the Thames yet, but I could invent stuff for the time being and then amend it in the light of what George came up with.

> I grew up near the Thames, but when I was little it was mostly invisible to me. My mum and me, we didn't get out a lot, not beyond the small park at the end of our road. And even though I had my camera, it wasn't to the Thames I went. I liked snapping birds, and loads came to feeders that Mum kept in the garden. I was more adventurous

when I was older and started going to the river. There were different birds there. Bigger and in some ways more interesting than the songbirds that came to the garden. Swans, geese, cormorants, herons. I was in heaven.

And one day another bird came along, a smasher of a bird that would change everything. I was mooching along the towpath when who should I see but local-girl-made-good, Kate Winslet. I asked her if could photograph her and she said yes, and I got some fabulous shots, one of which I sold for a tenner to the local rag!

Well, that was it. That was the start of my career. Professional photographer. I had worked in a camera shop after leaving school, and I'd learnt loads from the manager, a real diamond geezer who lent me different kinds of gear to experiment with and learn about.

Over the years I took photographs of the great and the good. And it paid the bills, make no mistake. But then, I thought – after some years, mind – that photographing celebrities was good for getting in the old spondulicks but was becoming a bit samey. I said to myself, 'George, me old mucker, you're getting stuck in a rut, son!'

So I decided to go back to where I had begun. I wanted to explore the River Thames, where I had taken my first professional photograph. I wanted to create a pictorial record of the social contrasts of this great waterway, this stunning river that springs up in the heart of England and broadens to an expanse of estuary that is a gateway to the rest of world.

I started in Reading, where I grew up. Over three weekends I explored the towpath between Mapledurham and Whitchurch. I was told that the more interesting houseboats would probably be further downstream. But the boating season was in full swing and I got the gist of the sort of people who use the river, from the canoeists to the rowers of skiffs, from the young families in day boats to the elderly couples in small cruisers. And, of course, the wealthy toffs, with their huge gin palaces.

It was on a gin palace that I took my first ride on the river, hitching a lift from Sonning Lock to Caversham Lock. And very comfortable it was! And I was even given a glass of expensive bubbly to sup!

River people are interesting. You see how relaxed the weekenders become, washing away the troubles of the week with the gentle pace of progress in the water. But the people I am really fascinated by are the houseboat dwellers. Not necessarily the ones who live in smart, state-of-the-art river homes on the outskirts of London and might just as well be living in flats. I am more interested in the people who have lived in beat-up old boats for yonks.

I banged this straight off to George by email, saying it was a five hundred-word start to his article, with a view to finding a voice that he felt was his. I was surprised that he emailed me back within the hour:

like it mate, strange to see me using proper puntuation and hifalutin stuff like a pictorial record of the social contrasts of this great waterway! not sure I'd ever use spondulicks, proberly dosh or evern lolly, also never say yonks, donkies ears maybe. but looking good!!

*

Later in the evening Luca rang. He was staying with Theresa in Hammersmith. She had been given some sedatives by her GP and was calmer now, but going over the accident again and again. He asked me for my account of how it had happened.

I told him of the great form his father had been in the previous evening. Of how thrilled Theresa had been at how well things had gone. I said that he had seemed in less good form in the morning, a little distracted, perhaps.

'After breakfast we decided to walk down to Hammersmith Broadway together and then go our separate ways. Theresa was just pointing out a restaurant to me and then, before we knew it, your father had wandered out into the road…He had no chance, Luca, I'm afraid…I'm so sorry, Luca, it's such a terrible way to go.' Luca was just listening, saying nothing. 'Please let me know if there is anything I can do. Anything at all… And give my love to Theresa. Tell her I'm thinking about her… thinking about you both.'

'Yes, Nick, I will… And thank you.'

*

Such a terrible way to go. So utterly terrible. I just couldn't get the images out of my head. The bus careering round the corner. Carlo's slowness in seeing it. His momentary surprise. His futile effort to fend it off with a raised hand. The slowly tumbling body arcing towards the tarmac and the wheels of the bus. A vivid, shocking, haunting moment, like watching a film in slow motion.

I remember being struck by the images of 9/11. The truly dreadful act of terrorism doesn't bear thinking about. And yet there is a filmic quality that somehow seems to soften the horror of the event, that lends it an air of make-believe, even a strange, unsettling kind of beauty: the second aircraft, slightly a-tilt, a silhouette against the lucid blue sky of a bright Manhattan morning, cuts into the east tower; the immediate aftermath, a rapidly dilating ball of flame and a slow-rising shroud of black smoke; the collapse of the west tower, neat, balletic, sinking smoothly and with an astonishing economy of movement to the ground beneath, leaving a rising white pall; the street-bound vortex of the gigantic dust-plume, a captured, enraged beast escaping, dynamic and shape-shifting, rounding a corner to pursue with ensnaring power the fleeing screaming crowd.

But there was nothing beautiful about the images of Carlo's last moments that played in my mind over and over again before I was finally able to lose myself in sleep.

10

When I awoke the next morning, it was with a dim sense of unease. Gradually, like blood seeping from a bandaged wound, the horror of the previous day came back to me.

I decided I would paint my study. I wanted to do something simple, something repetitive and relatively mindless. So I headed off to the local B&Q and spent a perplexing few minutes getting my head around the range of possible finishes and the huge assortment of subtly differing shades of paint. Some of the names were downright ridiculous, but it was the shade that mattered, not the name. I knew what I wanted and eventually settled on a large pot of something called Natural Calico Matt.

I shifted the furniture to the centre of the room, found an old sheet, sugar-soaped the walls and set to work, using a brush rather than a roller. There was something satisfying in dipping the brush into the pot to pick up exactly the right amount of paint: not so much so that it dripped on the dust sheet or ran down the wall; but enough for several evenly applied strokes.

In the past I had always found painting mind-numbingly boring, but of course it was precisely numbing the mind that I was now seeking, so I found the dull repetition deeply satisfying. Horizontal stroke, horizontal stroke, vertical stroke, vertical stroke. And the sound was pleasing, too, a rhythmic, gently abrasive whishing sound.

I made good progress and stopped for a cup of coffee when I was halfway through. There is always something unnerving in watching paint dry. The most recently applied paint always looks much darker than that applied earlier, and there are always wetter patches amongst the drier bits of wall where too much paint has been applied. The worry is that it will never dry into an even finish.

Watching paint dry has tended to receive a bad press. But as the morning wore on and I reached the final stretch, I looked with calm contentment on the drying wall I had started with.

Lying unopened on my desk was the ledger of Carlo's course notes which he had charmingly brought with him two days earlier as pledge of his future co-operation with me. As I recalled his willingness, his openness, his enthusiasm, I felt a sharp pang of loss. And a compulsion, a duty perhaps, to read it.

The early pages contained some general notes on the godfather of Cultural Studies, Richard Hoggart, who had founded the Birmingham Centre for Contemporary Cultural Studies in the early sixties. Broad areas of this new discipline are noted: Social Norms, Political Ideologies, High Culture, Popular Culture, Sub-culture, Feminism, Race. The interdisciplinary nature of Cultural Studies is emphasised in these opening pages of the ledger. The integrated arts – visual art, film, theatre, literature, music in all its forms – are noted to have a commonality in their relation to each other and to the people of a particular social grouping. The relationship between the press and television and their audiences is questioned: does the media influence or reflect popular culture, lead or follow? What are the customary historical effects of war on social norms and the integrated arts?

The general notes became more specific as Carlo began to home in on his real interest: the seismic cultural changes of the post-war years. Here Carlo lists topics he would perhaps like to lecture on:

The invention of the teenager
Teenage identity
Music
Fashion
Drugs
Morality
Look Back in Anger: rejection of the Establishment
Political radicalism
The Underground Press
Sub-cultures
Social practices of sub-groups in relation to dominant
    political and financial classes

I skimmed through the ledger. Carlo d'Abruzzi had inscribed his name neatly in the front cover, underneath which he had written a London address. In addition to the broad brush-stroke notes at the beginning, there was a reading list towards the end – either books he had read or intended to read, or a reading list for his future students. Books such as *Bomb Culture* by Jeff Nuttall, *Playpower* by Richard Neville, *The Politics of Ecstasy* by Timothy Leary and *The Neophiliacs* by Christopher Booker. After this list there were several pages of names and addresses, not in any particular order, as far as I could make out. But one name did leap out at me: Charlie Adams. Was this a reference to himself or not? The most intriguing pages were filled with doodles and tiny ink-drawn portraits, one of which looked like a self-portrait, although the name beneath was Alfonso. Beside this portrait, mysteriously, had been drawn what looked like some sticks of dynamite bound together elaborately with an axe head; I quickly realised that it was not sticks of dynamite at all, but a depiction of the emblem of the National Fascist Party of Italy.

But most of the ledger was filled with detailed topic notes; and these would have to wait, if indeed I was ever to read them.

*

Five days after Carlo's death I had a phone call from Luca. He told me that Theresa's deep sense of grief was mixed with a crippling sense of guilt, a sense that her father's death was her fault. If she had not looked away at the critical moment, Carlo would not have strayed into the road. But what was upsetting her most at the moment, he said, was the absence of any obituaries in the national press. There had been a paragraph in the *Evening Standard* and a brief report on the local television news about the accident, but both these had described him simply as a retired lecturer from Dorset, not as a man with an influential past.

'Nick, I hesitate to ask this, but she is wondering whether you could write something for one of the big dailies that would get the ball rolling. I know it is a big ask, but it would mean so much to her.'

I felt awkward. I was unsure whether, at this stage, I knew enough about the life of Carlo d'Abruzzi to write with any authority about him. To complicate things further, my contact with Fleet Street editors was largely either through my own agent or through the agents of my clients. 'Luca, I'm not sure I can do that… It's not that easy.' I explained to him my reservations and asked him to let me think about it some more.

He thanked me, said he would pass my comments on to his sister. I asked about the funeral, whether any arrangements had been made.

'It'll probably be in about a week, Nick. The coroner wanted an autopsy… I think they wanted to look at the state of Dad's brain to see if the dementia was a contributing factor to his death… And I gather also that the bus driver was arrested on suspicion of careless driving. I think some of the witnesses told the police that he was driving too fast around the corner.'

I asked him to let me know as soon as the funeral details were finalised and said I would be back to him about the article in a day or two.

In the evening I received another call. Theresa.

'Nick, it is so important that something is written about Papa… It's just so wrong that his passing is being ignored like this.' The voice was small and dull and hollow. She sounded exhausted, emotionally spent. I pictured her face, red and puffy, tired eyes with dark, baggy and bruised-looking skin beneath them.

'Theresa, my darling, I've thought about you so much. Felt your grief, shared your guilt. Not that it was your fault at all… I have not been in touch because… because I thought I would get in the way. I thought it best to leave you and Luca to grieve together.'

There was a sob. And then silence. And then a series of sharp, guttural cries. 'I'm sorry,' she said, and put the phone down.

*

An hour later the doorbell rang. It was Theresa.

'I had to see you, Nick, to talk this through. The article. You must do it, Nick, you are the only person who can.'

'Theresa, I told Luca I'd think about it… But, you see… I'm not sure if I know enough about your father to do a decent job—'

'Of course you do.' There was more animation in the voice than when she had been speaking on the phone. And, although she was looking tired, the face was not red or puffy or blotched as I had imagined. But she did look fragile, delicate; I wanted to hold her – gently, carefully, lovingly.

'And I'm not sure if any of the big editors would accept my piece.'

'Of course they would, Nick. He was a big man and you're a well-known writer.'

I gave a gentle laugh. 'I'm the invisible man, Theresa. I'm a ghost!'

And suddenly her face relaxed and she laughed, too. 'Woo! Very, very scary! …I could help you write the article. We could do it tomorrow!' Her characteristic enthusiasm, with its helter-skelter momentum, had resurfaced and was trumping, for the time being at any rate, her feelings of grief and guilt.

I asked her if she had eaten and she shook her head. 'Fancy a Chinese?' She nodded. So I picked up the phone and ordered a meal to be delivered to the house. While we were waiting, I printed off the piece I had written on Carlo's early childhood.

She wept as she read it, tears and shaking body threatening a collapse. She sat quietly for a moment after she had finished it and then, quite unexpectedly, came to me and kissed me wetly on the cheek. 'You're brilliant, Nick. That is absolutely wonderful!'

We chatted over the meal, Theresa affectionately raking over memories of her father at various stages of her life. There were no tears now. Giving form to her memories in words seemed to soothe her pain. We drank a little over half a bottle of wine, followed by coffee. And then I offered to walk her to the station.

She clutched my arm. 'Fuck me, Nick. Please fuck me. I want it. I need it.'

She was brittle and fragile and there seemed no point in refusing. We went upstairs, slowly got undressed and made love. There was an urgency, an intensity in her that was new, a complication of her grief perhaps; and her noisy climax seemed to sound a crescendo both of release and pain. We lay silently for about twenty minutes and then with a skilful hand she coaxed me gently into a repeat performance. For the first time we spent the whole night together.

*

In the morning I started writing the promised piece about Carlo. Before I did so, I rang Vikki, my agent, to see it she would be able to place it for me.

'But, Nick, why are you writing that if there is a whole book to come?'

I explained about the lack of obituaries – Vikki found this very odd – and suggested that putting the name out in the press would perhaps be good advance publicity. With my insistence on the urgency of the request, she suggested that I should perhaps talk to editors directly, explaining to them about Carlo and the value of my story.

So I emailed all the qualities and most of the red-tops, giving a brief account of Carlo, saying my piece was something between a feature and an obituary, adding that I was likely to go with the first paper which could offer me publication within the next three days. As it happened, it was *The Times* that came back to me, and within two hours, possibly because I knew the obituaries editor, for whom I had done some work in the past. By the time he confirmed that he would take the piece – as an obituary, naturally – I already had the article well underway. I also had two digital photographs that Theresa had scanned for me: the photo of Carlo at the Albert Hall Poetry Incarnation; and the presentation of the Waterford vase on the occasion of his retirement.

In the middle of the morning Luca rang Theresa to say the coroner was releasing the body. It seemed that the autopsy had suggested a brain with the expected signs and deterioration of ageing. The funeral could go ahead, a date had been fixed and the various arrangements made. Theresa immediately summarised the details so that announcements could be made in various newspapers:

The funeral service for Carlo d'Abruzzi will take place in Wimborne Minster at 11.30 a.m. on 6th June and will be followed by burial in Wimborne Cemetery.

Meanwhile, I completed my obituary and passed it to her for her approval:

THE MAN WHO CATALYSED THE 1960s
COUNTER-CULTURE

In November 1961, Brian Epstein, record-shop owner and future manager of the most famous band in history, was visited by a young man who had just landed in Liverpool docks after sailing from Hamburg. That man was Carlo d'Abruzzi. He was bringing word of a completely new sort of music which was being created in Hamburg by an unknown Liverpool group, the Beatles.

This seminal moment in Britain's post-war history was created by someone with a colourful past. Carlo d'Abruzzi was born in 1935 in Trieste, the grandson of Prince Umberto, Count of Salemi, and a descendent of Victor Emmanuel II, King of Italy. Trieste, in the late 1930s, was a troubled city. An historical fault-line between ethnic Italians and ethnic Slovenes was being further complicated by the increasing influence of neighbouring Germany. D'Abruzzi's young years in this fractious city would be scarred by two tragedies: the death of his mother in 1940 and the death of his father, in an air crash, a year later. Fortunately, the young boy had a nanny who had contacts in England. Thus, after a long and dangerous trek across Europe, the pair found refuge with foster parents, farmers in west Devon. Here he would find the happy and secure environment that he had hitherto lacked.

Perhaps it was his cosmopolitan background which prompted this bright boy to go to university in America rather than in Britain. A Liberal Arts degree at Columbia University in New York was followed by an adventurous spell as a merchant sailor. Fortuitously, one of his voyages would take him to Hamburg, where he would discover the Beatles.

After accompanying Epstein to his first Beatles lunch-time concert in the Cavern Club, d'Abruzzi headed for London. Here he would find that young people were waking up from the dreary slumber of the post-war years in search of something new. They were rejecting the ordinances of their parents' generation and wanted to create for themselves a new sense of identity. They wanted their own music, their own fashion, their own politics and their own morality. While Prime Minister Harold Wilson was talking about the white heat of technology, young people were forging their own technicolour dreams in the crucible of 1960s London.

And it was at the heart of much of this change – revolution, some might call it – that Carlo d'Abruzzi was to be found. Social historians who identify the key moments of change – the key 'happenings', to use a favourite word of the sixties – will find the fingerprint of d'Abruzzi on almost all of them.

It might be difficult today to believe that the Albert Hall could be filled to the dome with young people coming together to listen to an entire evening of poetry readings. And it might be difficult to imagine a significant number of that audience smoking dope, while others tripped out on acid. But this is what happened. On 11th June 1965, the International Poetry Incarnation was held. Amongst the performers were Allen Ginsberg, Gregory Corso, Lawrence Ferlinghetti, William Burroughs and some well-known young British poets. Earlier in the month d'Abruzzi had attended a poetry reading by Allen Ginsberg at Better Books on Charing Cross Road. After the event he had suggested to Ginsberg that it would be good to arrange a much bigger event and, when asked what the biggest venue in London might be, d'Abruzzi had said the Albert Hall and had proceeded to book it. To the architects of the counter-culture, this momentous event signalled the possibility of real and continuing change; it would be the precursor to other extraordinary landmark happenings of the decade.

The underground culture in London had an astonishing energy, but there was something fragmentary about it. While philosophies and anti-establishment views were broadly shared, subsets tended to group together around their interests, such as fashion, or literature, or music or left-wing politics, or feminism.

With the intention of prompting these different subsets to talk to each other, to cross-fertilise ideas, d'Abruzzi in 1966 came up with the idea of an underground newspaper that would provide a platform and voice for these disparate groups. That platform was a paper, the famous *International Times* or *it*, as it carried on its masthead. *it* was published from a small office in Southampton Row, attracting an eclectic range of contributors who wrote on a variety of topics. Music, art and fashion were well represented, as were local issues such as scrapping pub-licensing laws, making London an all-night city, with tubes running twenty-four hours a day; advice was offered on such things as drugs and sex and squatting in unoccupied houses; and it had a strong political edge, calling for the cessation of the Vietnam War, opposing apartheid in South Africa and arguing the feminist cause. For the launch, by all accounts a truly Bacchanalian evening, d'Abruzzi hired the Roundhouse at Chalk Farm, a decrepit barn of a building. A friend of his persuaded Pink Floyd to perform at the event.

Always at the cutting edge, and keen to drive things forward, d'Abruzzi would, two years later, return to the Roundhouse to promote an historic dusk-to-dawn concert with The Doors and Jefferson Airplane. This single event was notable for introducing to this country of one of the edgiest rock bands in the world, and for preparing the way for London to become an all-night city.

But by the end of the decade the mood was souring. To some, the beginning of the end was marked by the murders at The Rolling Stones'

Altamont concert in the USA in 1969; to others it was the drug-fuelled killings by the Manson family. Meanwhile, in London, poor organisation and poor financial management saw the slow demise of the *International Times*. For Carlo d'Abruzzi, it was time to up sticks and move on. An Institute for Higher Education in a sleepy seaside town on the south coast was looking for someone to set up a Contemporary Cultural Studies course. D'Abruzzi, an ideal fit, applied for the position, was awarded it, and remained in post until his retirement in 2000, by which time the institution had been elevated first to a polytechnic and finally to a university.

D'Abruzzi married Brenda Lewin in 1978. In 1990 the couple had twins, Theresa and Luca, who brought much comfort to their father after the premature death of Brenda in 1999. He enjoyed a modest retirement, mindful of his influential past in the turbulent decade of the 1960s, but content to enjoy a quiet country life in Dorset.

Carlo d'Abruzzi, a significant figure in the cultural revolution of 1960s Britain, was born on 17 January 1935. He died on 8 June 2015, aged 80.

Theresa liked the piece, so I emailed it off to *The Times*. Little would either of us guess how enormous the consequences would be.

PART II

LINES OF ENQUIRY

11

My article in *The Times* was published the day before Carlo's funeral, a day I shall never forget. I was pleased with the job the copy editor had done. Although he had dispensed with my headline, preferring to run with *The Man Who Invented the Sixties*, he had laid out the article well and given suitable prominence to the photo of Carlo at the Albert Hall Poetry Incarnation. Theresa had, of course, rushed out early to buy several copies of the paper, and had rung me excitedly to say what a good job they had done, and how grateful she was for the wonderful piece I'd written.

And that, really, should have marked an end-point: an important life suitably obituarised and suitably commemorated by the funeral service the following day. A fitting end to the eventful life of Carlo d'Abruzzi.

But in fact it was at precisely this moment, in the aftermath of his death, his shocking, unforgettable death, that the real story of Carlo d'Abruzzi begins.

*

I drove down to Wimborne on the eve of Carlo's funeral. By the time I had checked in to my hotel in the town square, I already had three missed calls from Robert Wainwright, the obituaries editor of *The Times*. And when I checked my phone I saw that he had forwarded to me several emails, most containing Carlo's name in the title. The phone message, left after his third unanswered call, was short and sweet: 'Nick, we need to talk. There appear to be some problems with the d'Abruzzi piece.' Once I had sorted myself out in the hotel room, I skimmed the emails. There clearly was a problem. One of the emails was from a prominent activist in the 1960s; another was from a daughter of the author, now dead, of one of the most vivid and telling personal testimonies of the decade; a third was from a social historian of the period. All had written to say that Carlo d'Abruzzi was a name they were not familiar with; and to suggest that many of the achievements ascribed to him in my obituary were actually the achievements of other people.

I felt a deep dread as I read these messages. I had spent years building up my reputation as a reliable writer, a dealer in truth rather than supposition or fantasy. Although my obituary had appeared without a by-line in *The Times*, I knew that there was the danger that some gossip would surface about me. Fleet Street is a small, incestuous world. I worried that word would get round that I was no longer reliable, that I didn't check my facts. And, of course, I hadn't.

I now deeply regretted my involvement with Theresa. I had known, when I had first slept with her, that I was contaminating a professional relationship, and yet I had weakly allowed it to continue. And, worst of all, that closeness to her – my unquestioning responsiveness to her emotional needs – had prompted me to write an article, the obituary, that I knew in my heart I was not really equipped to write.

And yet, here I was in Wimborne Minster, a sleepy market town, preparing to accompany Theresa to the burial of her father. So I emailed Robert Wainwright to say I was away from my office, down in Wimborne to attend d'Abruzzi's funeral, that I would get back to him as soon as possible.

*

It was a short walk from my hotel to the minster church, an impressive building dating back to Saxon times. I had not seen either Theresa or Luca for a few days. I knew that they were staying in Carlo's house nearby, from where they had been making arrangements for the funeral.

The church was almost empty when I arrived. Two middle-aged couples sitting with younger people – nephews and nieces and grand-nephews and grand-nieces of Brenda, I assumed. Huddled together was another small group of people, looking as though they might be former university colleagues, but I couldn't really tell. However, apart from one or two in this group, there was no one of Carlo's age, none of his 1960s contemporaries, as far as I could see. This surprised me and, as I glanced around the minster, with row upon row of empty pews, I was sure that the first thing to strike Theresa as she entered the church would be size of the congregation. And I was equally sure that she would be deeply disappointed.

The funeral party processed up the nave, its slow progress accompanied by the organ arrangement of an extract from

Berlioz's *Requiem*. Luca, face impassive, was carrying in his hand what I assumed to be his eulogy to his father. Next to him, on his arm, was Theresa. She was veiled, and through the wide mesh of lace I could see that she looked terribly fragile: her pale face was staring steadfastly ahead, and in her body and in her gait there was a stiffness, making every small step appear laboured and awkward. I hoped that she would manage to keep herself together.

A greeting from the rector offered a special welcome to newcomers to the town. And then there were a few words about Carlo. About his work at the university and about his love of the local area. Soon it was time for Luca to deliver his eulogy. He was a lawyer, used to presenting himself to audiences, so naturally he spoke with considerable confidence; and without, in fact, looking at the notes he had brought with him. He mentioned Carlo's Italian background and the war-time flight to Britain. There was a warmth to his voice, especially as he talked about the father of his own childhood. What was strange, though, was the way he seemed to gloss over what one would presume to have been the most interesting years of Carlo's life, the 1960s. He said something like, 'They say that, if you can remember the sixties, you weren't there. Well, Dad was there. And he did remember them. And, by all accounts, had a pretty wild time before settling down to become a respectable lecturer in this lovely part of the country.'

The small congregation was not very tuneful, so there was something a little desultory about its singing of 'Abide with Me' and 'Lord of All Hopefulness'. The thinness of sound was quickly swallowed by the vast hollows of the minster. And soon the great edifice was emptied of its tiny gathering, the main party heading for the cemetery, a short distance away. As the coffin was carried up the aisle to the waiting hearse, with Theresa slowly following behind, I had my first real view of her face. She bore a dignified look of restraint, the pain and the sorrow temporarily held in check; there was a nod here and there to someone she knew; and she even managed a tiny smile as she walked past me, catching my eye.

Approached by a narrow lane and contained within iron railings, the cemetery lay on the side of a gently sloping hill that climbed out of the town. Not all of those who had attended the funeral service came to the cemetery, so it was a small gathering around the grave, with one or two hanging back at a distance to give space to Luca and Theresa. As in the minster, there was a sense of smallness, of being lost in something larger, this tiny group gathered under the large dome of blue sky with its few ragged streaks of cloud.

It was as Theresa threw the trowel of earth onto the lowered coffin that the dam of grief finally burst, splintering the stillness and dignity she had shown until then. Luca put his arms around her, with little effect. She wailed and sobbed and heaved without restraint, the sounds rasping and catching and wheezing, and it was terrible to hear.

I bowed my head as the noise continued and then looked away. And couldn't believe what I saw. Beyond a railing that marked the boundary of the cemetery, and partly hidden behind a yew tree, was George Nelson, long-lens camera in hand. I rushed over to him, half walking, half running, sweeping my arm in a gesture of dismissal as I approached him.

'Get the fuck out of here, you little shit,' I said. 'How dare you intrude on this sad event, you heartless ghoul.'

George said nothing. He puckered his mouth, shrugged his shoulders as if to say, 'What's your problem, mate?' and headed off down the narrow cemetery road.

*

I did not attend the small reception for mourners that was held back at Carlo's house; I had told Luca that I would be in touch in due course. When the burial service was complete I said my farewells and headed back to Kingston.

More forwarded emails had arrived during the day. As I read through them – they came from a variety of sources – I began to build up a picture of the problem. It seemed an undisputed fact that it was Bill Harry, founder and editor of the Liverpool music paper, *Mersey Beat*, who had introduced Brian Epstein to the Beatles; it was he who had taken Epstein to his first lunch-time concert in November 1961. While no one denied that Carlo d'Abruzzi had attended the Albert Hall Poetry Incarnation – the evidence of Theresa's prized photograph was incontrovertible – a number of people, including the author of the seminal social history of the 1960s, declared that it was Tony Godwin, founder of Better Books, who was the pivotal figure in the event. Similarly, there was widespread agreement that it was John Hopkins and Barry Miles – both well-documented figures of the cultural revolution of the 1960s – who had founded *International Times*. And it was likely that Hopkins was the promoter or co-promoter of The Doors concert at the Roundhouse in 1968.

The most significant email, the most disappointing and potentially the most damaging, was from Robert Wainwright himself, which opened with a clumsily tasteless comment, in the light of the way Carlo had died:

Nick,

Your obit on d'Abruzzi was car-crash journalism. Many of your ascribed facts were unchecked and just plain wrong – sloppy stuff. I had expected better from you. From what I can gather, it is nonsense to suggest that your man introduced Epstein to the Beatles, that he founded *it*, that he set up the big Albert Hall poetry event and that he brought The Doors to this country. I am waiting for someone to write in to tell me he was never a university lecturer...

We're going to have to run a fairly lengthy corrections paragraph in a day or two and no doubt in the letters Ed will include some of the correspondence he has received.

You are lucky that at this paper we still publish most of our obits without a by-line. Your reputation, therefore, is not as damaged as it might otherwise have been. But please, Nick, do look into this to see how you got it all so wrong.

As ever,
Rob

*

'Just me? No Theresa?' Luca said as we sat down.

I was meeting him in a smart coffee bar in the city. I knew that I had to alert Theresa and Luca to the corrections that *The Times* would soon be publishing. And I dreaded the response that would greet this news – at least from Theresa. So I had rung Luca to ask him if we could meet for lunch or coffee, whichever suited.

'The thing is, Luca, that we have a bit of a problem. No doubt it will upset you... but I think it will devastate Theresa.' I explained to him about the furore the obituary had precipitated.

There was a long, long pause, Luca raising his head a little, his eyes moving in a deliberative manner. 'To be honest, Nick, I am not wholly surprised. I don't know if you remember but, when we first met at Theresa's flat for dinner, I did try to warn you that dad loved to tell a good story. I was never wholly convinced, I don't why. But Theresa... Theresa loved his tales ...He was always closer to Tease than me... I wonder... perhaps his tales were for her, mainly for her... perhaps just for her. I don't know. He was always closer to Theresa but, having said that, in the last couple of years we did have some interesting chats. And with virtually every conversation I got this increasing sense that he was carrying some sort of burden... some sort of burden from his early life... And that he wanted to be free of it.'

I didn't interrupt. Of course I remembered Luca's warning about his storytelling father, and I realised now just how fully I had been led by Theresa into her version of her father.

He carried on. 'I don't think he liked the idea of your book. In so far as he co-operated with you, it was to please

Theresa – he doted on her.' I nodded. 'One of the most relaxed conversations I had with him in recent years was one of our last, only a few weeks ago... He said a strange thing. He said... he was enjoying rediscovering himself... getting to know himself... again.'

'That is interesting. What do you think he meant?'

'I really don't know, Nick. But I wondered if he had been escaping something all his life.'

'But that, of course, is true... The flight from Trieste.'

'Hmmmm—'

'You think that wasn't true?'

'I don't know. I really don't know.'

'So what should we do, Luca? Should I abandon the book or get stuck into deeper research? ...And if the latter, how will Theresa take it?'

'Not well.' And then he said very decisively, 'Look, the three of us have got to meet together and talk this through. I'll arrange something and get back to you.'

*

We met the following weekend in Hammersmith. By this stage, an official correction had already appeared in *The Times*. Tactfully it did not say that my account of Carlo's influence in the 1960s was a load of tosh, but it did say that the obituary had exaggerated his impact on the decade; and it rightly gave credit to the true shapers of those interesting times.

Only two letters appeared in the letters column. One was from the author of the authoritative 950-page account of the 1960s, who reeled off the names of the real catalysts of the counter-culture, the Alternative Society. The other was from a colleague writing about Carlo's days as a lecturer. She spoke of Carlo's considerable knowledge of his subject and his powerful way of communicating with young minds. The tone was admiring and affectionate, a refreshing corrective to the indignant emails that Robert Wainwright had forwarded to me.

*

Luca had texted me as I was on my way to Hammersmith to say that Theresa was aware of *The Times* correction and letters, but he gave no indication of her response.

Coming out of the tube station was difficult. Everything seemed so normal: the dull drone of the traffic broken sporadically by the throaty roar of a motorbike or the blare of a horn; the frantic speed at which everybody seemed to be moving. There was no indication of the terrible personal tragedy that had occurred on this busy piece of road the previous month. There had been a brief hiatus. And then quickly the life of this community had moved purposefully forward once more, like the waves of the sea closing swiftly and inexorably above a wreck that has dropped down deep to the seabed below.

When I arrived at Theresa's flat, she greeted me without any real warmth and offered me a cup of coffee. The three of us quickly got down to business. Luca was matter-of-fact. There was his lawyer's logic in the way he looked at the matter. He outlined the problem. That I had been commissioned to write a book. The premise of the book was that my subject was a notable man of considerable achievement. That it was the detail of this life which would make the book interesting and sellable. That this detail had now been proved to be false. That, with the point of book removed, it was questionable whether I should proceed with the project.

'So,' he said, 'the question, Tease, is whether we should ask Nick to stand down. Pay him off, if necessary… Or whether we should ask him to continue with the project, but with a different emphasis. That we should ask him to continue with his researches. Dig away to get at the truth of Dad's life. Then we can decide how we might want to act upon it.'

I nodded, waiting for Theresa to speak. But she remained silent, so Luca continued. 'My inclination is to opt for the latter course. Nick, you would do whatever you saw fit. We would give you all the help you needed.'

I nodded once more.

'You won't find anything much different,' Theresa said. 'The most you'll find is that he used a different name in the 1960s… For the reasons I have already told you.' There was a sharpness in her voice. Her manner wasn't exactly hostile, but there was hint of challenge in it. She had lost her trust in me; no longer saw me as her collaborator on the sacred quest properly to memorialise her father. Or that was how it seemed. I thought she was being a little unfair on me. It was she, after all, who had pressured me into writing something for the papers. And yet… I should have been professional enough to resist. It had been utter folly to offer an improperly researched obituary for publication.

'If you are both keen for me to look into your father's early life, I am happy to do it. But you will have to give me freedom to follow up all the avenues that present themselves.

135

And I'll need, at some early stage, I'm afraid, to look at the materials in his study.'

'That's fine,' Luca said. Theresa nodded, without looking me in the eye.

So it was agreed. And it seemed that my role now, an unfamiliar one, had been elevated from one of mere researcher to that of detective. It was not something I was completely happy with. The time I spent investigating the identity of Carlo d'Abruzzi would not earn me any money; or at least there had not been any mention of payment. But I felt obliged. An obligation to Theresa and Luca. And more importantly an obligation towards myself. For the first time in my career I had allowed a shoddy piece of work to be published. Thankfully it was not in my name; but it stung, nevertheless, and I wanted to prove to myself – and to Robert Wainwright, of course – that I could make good my errors. I wanted to find out who the real Carlo d'Abruzzi was.

12

I've long been fascinated by what exactly constitutes 'a person'. I am not a philosopher, I'm a jobbing writer, and I suspect it is my particular line of work, the kind of writing that I do, that has given me this abiding interest in the nature of identity. My proximity to people in the public eye has enabled me to observe first-hand the difficulties that some celebrities experience over their own sense of self, the problem frequently lying in the disconnect between the public image and their own sense of who they are. The perceived image, after all, has been constructed by other people, the managers and publicists and the public with whom they are in collusion.

My impression is that few people, when they set out on their journey to fame, fortune and celebrity, have any real of idea of what they are heading towards. They like the idea of good money, of recognition, of being admired and loved, of being validated. And on a small scale this is probably fine: a comfortable standard of living, double-takes in the street, the occasional request to pose with a stranger for a selfie. The persona of someone like this is a carapace, a mask, something removable. For some, the mask moulds closely and accurately to the face. When it is taken off, the face is recognisable. For others, whilst the mask may distort, disguise or exaggerate certain features, the recognisable person emerges when it is removed.

But what happens when your public persona, the confected character imposed on you by your fame, the finely fashioned mask, becomes more and more distant, more alien from who you once were, leaving the real you lost somewhere between the public person and the half-forgotten you? And what if the public person does not become too distant, but instead grows huge and heavy and irremovable; when ownership of it is finally and completely taken from you by a public which created you and defines you now by its demands and expectations? Who are you, then? And where do you live? You have to learn to live as your alter ego in the cage of celebrity, weighted with a gilded ball and chain of fame. Or perhaps you seek escape by becoming a recluse, hidden from view, filing away at the chain around your ankle, hoping to break free and rediscover yourself. But then even if you tuck yourself away, you will almost certainly have parasites like George Nelson hunting you down.

Identity for most people is straightforward. The components of your identity are various and you offer the different elements, these mosaic-like pieces, in different patterns and different combinations to others, hoping – but never knowing – that they see these carefully selected facets as you see them yourself. This is how you keep hold of a reasonably comfortable sense of self, believing, falsely perhaps, that you are in control, that you are the only person who knows all the variants of self, the only person who can unite them into a single understanding, a coherent entity.

So – and this is really where this has all been leading – who was Carlo d'Abruzzi? What collection of façades, what series of inventions, personalities, and performances inhered in that name? And for whom? The identity of Carlo d'Abruzzi to his students was of a kind man who wanted to share his extensive knowledge. The identity of Carlo d'Abruzzi to an admiring daughter was a person of royal descent and a person of considerable national achievement. And nested within that Carlo d'Abruzzi was Papa, a loving father who parented his children caringly. But who was Carlo d'Abruzzi to his inventor? Was he the carefully crafted persona who allowed the man, the boy refugee, to escape his fearful past? Whatever the persona had been in the past, Luca had suggested that his father had, in his final years, been keen to shed an identity he was no longer comfortable with, like a snake sloughing off a skin that it had outgrown.

Then again, perhaps Carlo's worries about who he was simply reflected a sense of self that was slipping from him due to the slow onset of dementia. His identity as Prince Carlo had slipped anchor, and now he was riding choppy, confused waters where he muddled, for example, the names of Rosa and Maria in his ancestry. But there were still fixed bearings: he retained the identity of the loving father, conferred on him by Theresa. That, too, of course, would have gone if he had lived to experience the completed decline into full dementia, when all the facets, the façades of identity would eventually have dissolved into a sad vacancy. Who we are is contingent upon the porous vessel of memory, which holds our histories, which gives us remembered ways of being, of talking, of behaving.

As I say, I am no philosopher. But an enquirer, yes. And wanting to find out who Carlo d'Abruzzi was.

I hoped that I would indeed find out. I needed to find out. My quest had become even more urgent. Ten days after Carlo's funeral, the latest edition of *Private Eye* had hit the streets and doormats, carrying a cruel piece in its 'Street of Shame' section that reduced me to a figure of fun. It was headed 'Taking the O out of Count':

> If you have never heard of Count Carlo d'Abruzzi, then you are not alone. Despite a fulsome obituary in *The Times* describing him as the man who introduced Epstein to the Beatles and the brains behind all kinds of important events in the social revolution of the 1960s, it seems that not many other people have heard of the man either. Especially the real architects of the sixties revolution and their chroniclers, who wrote in their droves to *The Times's* obituaries editor, Robert Wainwright. It seems that d'Abruzzi was a humble polytechnic lecturer in Cultural Studies, not the cultural icon of the swinging sixties that he claimed to be.
>
> And who rehashed these absurd claims in his overblown obituary? Step forward one Nick Barry, ghostwriter to the stars. Well, poor Nick, the ghost in the machine, so to speak, is no longer pale as a ghost, he is very red-faced indeed, and he is trying very hard to lay the ghost of his egregious error. Not that he has the ghost of a chance. He might

as well give up the ghost and forget about future commissions.

*

I was back in Wimborne, booked into the hotel I had stayed the night before Carlo's funeral. I had arranged to meet Theresa at Carlo's house the next morning. Unlike her father himself, she was happy for me to go through whatever I wanted in his study. He had been cagey when I had visited earlier in the year: the hostile, defensive look, the refusal to share any of his books, keeping me at arm's length.

So it was the books I started with, the ones that were written in the sixties or early seventies, which were contemporary accounts rather than social histories. I was interested in four in particular: *Bomb Culture* by Jeff Nuttall, *Playpower* by Richard Neville, *The Politics of Ecstasy* by Tim Leary and *A Cellarful of Noise* by Brian Epstein. All were heavily annotated, scrawled with underlinings, double-underlinings and marginal notes. The most interesting of the latter were bits of text – a phrase, a sentence, a whole paragraph – marked with asterisks; and almost always the asterisked sections had 'Cd'A' written by them. As I skimmed through the books, slowing to read the bits marked in this particular way, I began to realise that they contained phrases and sentences that I was familiar with. And I realised, too, that it was a familiarity that came from my conversations with Carlo and from listening to the tapes of his interviews with Theresa. Of course, a lecturer would very readily commit to memory pieces of information that would be useful in his teaching. But I increasingly had the feeling – no more than a hunch at this stage – that these marked gobbets formed part of the patchwork coat in which Carlo had dressed himself for his 1960s incarnation.

It was strange being in the house. There was that stillness and sadness that can inhabit places after their main presence has been removed. Fortunately, Theresa was being friendly enough. Gone was the sharpness of manner which she had shown the last time we had met. But there remained a coolness. Or a coolness, certainly, when compared to the warm, wildly enthusiastic young woman I had worked with before her father's death. And that, of course, was the point, I suppose. That she was grieving: struggling with every simple task, struggling to fall asleep at night, struggling desperately to keep hold of a sense of something, however small, to look forward to. I remember when my mother died. For months I had this feeling of being submerged, a heaviness, a dimness of perception. This is what I was seeing in Theresa. She looked so vulnerable that I wanted to take her in my arms, soothe her, cocoon her. I wanted to protect her in the weakness of her grief and help her until she got stronger.

We broke for a coffee mid-morning.

'There's so much to sort out upstairs,' she said.

'I can imagine. And I think you'll probably find the study a bit of a challenge.'

'Yes… I don't think Papa ever threw anything away!'

'But there's no huge rush to sort everything out, is there?' She shook her head. There was a short silence and then, '…How are you getting on at work?' I asked hesitantly.

'To be honest, it's the only thing that keeps me sane. It's a distraction… It's a godsend at the moment.'

I asked her if she really was happy that I was poking around in her father's past. 'Or are you doing this more for Luca than for yourself? Would you rather I wasn't here, going through your father's stuff?'

'I don't know, Nick. I don't know what I want. Luca once told me that he thought there was something fishy about Grandpa, Victor... He thought that Victor might have been a German spy reporting back to the Reich on dissident movements in Trieste. But I don't know why he thought that. As far as I know, there was not the slightest bit of evidence. And anyway, Papa was a lovely man, a successful man. I know that Luca had doubts about some of his stories... and if they turn out to be exaggerated – or untrue, even, some of them – then that's the way it is. It won't alter the way I see him... my memories of him.'

I put my hand over hers. There was nothing sexual in the gesture. It was one of reassurance, a kind of sealing of a pact that we would go forward together in our search for the truth.

I told her about the annotations and about my suspicions, insensitive and unwise, perhaps, in her current state. I had always been aware that she and her father had the same wonderful smile. And now, for the first time, I saw that she also had his same glare of hostile defensiveness. But the face quickly relaxed. She nodded and said I had to do what I had to do.

When I returned to the study I decided I would go through the large pedestal desk. It was a handsome piece, its polished wood and buffed leather top suggesting it had been well looked after. Beneath the gleam, it looked lived-in, so to speak, with the tell-tale signs of long and useful service – the dinks in the woodwork, the ink-stained and worn patches of green leather.

Much of what was to be found in or on the desk were the functional things one might expect to find: a drawer of pens, pencils, highlighters; another with the paraphernalia of banking; another with stationery of various size and types. The bottom right drawer was double-sized and contained, the spines facing upwards, ledgers like the one Carlo had given me, his lecture notes spanning the years.

I felt at my most intrusive when I examined the contents of the larger central drawer, which contained an untidy collection of personal letters and cards. Looking randomly at some of the dates, I could see that they stretched back a fair way, fifteen years and more. There was a hand-written letter from the vice-chancellor of his university, written on the occasion of Carlo's retirement. It was full of warmth and gratitude for the 'hugely significant contribution you have made to this institution over many years, and the unstinting help you have always given to fellow staff and, very particularly, to students'. Lying on the top, towards the back of the drawer, was a Father's Day card. The image on the front was a touching photograph of Carlo and Theresa holding hands against the backdrop of a stretch of water with hills behind. She looked about nine or ten, was gazing admiringly up towards her father whose face radiated a sense of complete happiness. 'To Dad…' was printed in large orange letters on the sky above the hills, and inside, above Theresa's hand-written inscription with its multitude of kisses, was '… the very bestest dad in all the whole wide world'.

On the wall above the desk was a large hessian-covered pin-board. A few of the pinned attachments were practical:

a plumber's card; details of a hospital appointment to see a consultant neurologist; a colourful 1:25,000 Ordnance Survey map marked out with a walk to Badbury Rings, a few miles outside Wimborne. But most were decorative: a large postcard of a country road running through a long avenue of mature beech trees; an A4-sized picture of a wide-eyed frog, with its head above water; next to it a flyer for a novel called *A Parcel of Fortunes* by an author I had never heard of.

Two of the walls were lined with shelves, weighted with books lying in an untidy geometry of shapes. In the niches either side of a chimney breast and fireplace there were shallow cupboards, with more bookshelves above.

It was to the cupboards that I turned my attention next. One was peeping open from the great wodge of papers that was beginning to spill out. A quick search of these revealed them to be almost exclusively about the house: deeds, mortgage papers, remortgage papers, repair bills, furniture bills, refurbishment invoices, household accounts; but nothing that yielded any clues to the earlier identity of Carlo d'Abruzzi.

The other cupboard, standing beneath shelves over-packed haphazardly and non-alphabetically with fiction, was locked. Unable to locate a key, I went to find Theresa, who was now preparing lunch in the kitchen, but she didn't know where it was. So I went back to the desk and searched again through the drawers. Nothing. On the desk-top there was a lamp, a leather tub for pens which I emptied, a small tray filled with jotting paper – I emptied this too – and a small, hollow brass Buddha. As I picked this up it made a clink. And there it was. A key. The key. The Open Sesame to what would perhaps contain interesting pointers to Carlo's past and to my future investigations.

*

The afternoon began with Theresa popping out to the shops, saying she would be back by mid-afternoon, leaving me to explore the unlocked cupboard and make a remarkable find, which I excitedly showed Theresa on her return. It was a children's book, *The Royal Families of Europe*. The corners of the cover were bumped and the spine was loose, but the pages within, apart from a few dog-eared ones, were intact and very charming in a simple sort of way: the illustrations of people and places simply drawn and boldly coloured; the type large, with small amounts of text to each page. This edition of the book had been published in 1939. The opening section, on the British monarchy and with a picture of a young Princess Elizabeth barely in her teens, looked well-thumbed.

But most interesting, and even more thumbed, was the section on the Italian monarchy. And tucked away in the back cover was an old, creased page of quarto-sized lined paper, the left-hand edge suggesting it had been torn from a jotter pad with a spiral binder. It contained, in the small and carefully formed writing of a child, a family tree. Carlo's family tree.

The page was top heavy, filled with the names of the forebears of Carlo's father, Victor d'Abruzzi. Victor's father was shown as Umberto, Count of Salemi, his mother Catherine Theresa of Aosta. It was mostly the ancestors of Umberto who appeared to have interested Carlo. I traced my finger along Carlo's neatly drawn lines of lineage.

Umberto was the son King Amadeo I of Spain, who had married Maria Letizia Bonaparte, whose own father, Prince Napoleon, was a nephew of the great Napoleon Bonaparte. Victor Emmanuel II, King of Italy, appeared in the pedigrees of both Amadeo and Maria Letizia, illustrating the characteristic inbreeding of European royals. Kingdoms and dukedoms of Europe are spread liberally amongst this network of families: Spain, Italy, Austria, Württemberg, Savoy, Aosta, Sardinia, Tuscany.

The tree spread from the top right almost to the edge of the left margin of the page. Poignantly, no antecedents were shown for Maria, Carlo's mother, which is why the page appeared top heavy: the bottom third was blank. And then, squashed onto the page, almost falling off the left-hand side, Carlo had written his own name and above it drawn a sketch of a little stick man with a crude crown!

When I showed this page to Theresa, she smiled a flash of sunshine. 'Aah,' she said, 'that's so cute!' She stared at it for a long, long time, delighted with the find. And while she looked at this excavated piece of her father's history, I looked at her. As she leant over the desk, touching this aged sheet of jotting paper, feeling a connection – a communication perhaps – with her dead father, there was a loveliness to her that I would have longed to capture had I been a painter. For a moment, the pinched face of grief had softened into an expanded radiance of joy.

The other interesting item in the cupboard was a slim cardboard folder. At the front were some newspaper clippings, job advertisements from 1969 and 1970. Two were for university libraries – Southampton and the recently chartered University of Sussex. A third was for the post at the Institute of Higher Education to which Carlo would eventually be appointed. They were looking for a teacher of Contemporary Cultural Studies as part of a team to introduce this new discipline. The advertisement stated that the successful applicant would be involved in designing the course, the words emphatically underlined – presumably by Carlo – in heavy red ink.

There was no CV in the file, but there were three letters: a typed carbon copy of Carlo's letter of application, an invitation for interview in January 1970, and a letter of appointment, which recorded how much the interviewing panel had enjoyed meeting Carlo and how pleased they were at his suitability for the role. It would be beneficial for the institute to have a lecturer with an American Liberal Arts degree, and it would be useful to have someone helping to design the course who had Carlo's insider knowledge of some of the great movements of the 1960s.

The letter of application was perhaps the most interesting find. It drew attention to the relevance of his Columbia degree, and stated, of course, his deep interest in the subject, outlining his various involvements in the counter-culture and his wide reading on the subject. But what was news, both to me and to Theresa, was that he had spent the previous three years working as a librarian at the Brixton Public Library; the chief librarian, the letter said, would be happy to be contacted for a reference. And the letter, of course, was headed with an address, a flat or a room in Herne Hill, a short distance away from his work at the library.

13

When I rang the library to ask if they kept old employment records, I was told by the senior librarian that they would have nothing going back as far as the 1960s and that it was unlikely that Lambeth council would have anything from that time either. Just as I was about end the call the man said, 'Hang on a minute. There's a nice old lady who used to work here back in the day. She is retired now, but comes in several days a week and occasionally helps out as a volunteer. Old habits, etc., etc., as they say… Molly Dibben, she's called. If you give me your number, I can ask her if she'd give you a call. She might remember the person you're enquiring after.'

Sure enough, later in the day, Molly rang me, clearly intrigued. When I told her that I was researching the life of Carlo d'Abruzzi, she let out a squawk of pleasure.

'Carlo! Gosh, yes, I remember Carlo so well. Adorable man… And very dishy, too!' she said with an uninhibited laugh.

*

Molly – I assumed it was Molly – was chatting to a librarian behind the tall loans desk. She looked at me expectantly and smiled, stepping forward with an outstretched hand. 'Mr Barry?'

'Molly?' We shook hands. 'It's Nick.'

She was a short, stout woman with sparkly eyes and a jolly face, aged, I would guess, in her early seventies. Her hair, some black amongst the mainly white, was long and plaited into two neat ponytails. She moved briskly and gave the sense of someone who looked out onto the world with optimism and with a considerable generosity of spirit. I felt sure that she would be able to give me a good account of Carlo. On my way to the library I had noticed a coffee shop next door, the Ritzy, so I suggested we go there for our chat.

'So, Nick, you are researching into Carlo's life. What fun! I never did hear of him again after he left the library. He said he was off to be a university librarian somewhere, I don't remember where. But him I remember very well.'

'Did you work together at the library for a long time?'

'Well, we didn't actually work together to begin with. I was a junior librarian, not long out of college, and he – he was a few years older than me – he used to come into the library and spend hours browsing. He was a very striking figure. Long hair, very handsome face – film starrish, I would say' – she half giggled – 'and very fashionably dressed. Very! Like a peacock… Do you remember that song? *A Dedicated Follower of Fashion*? …No, probably too young. But like that! And such a nice man—'

'Nice in what way?'

'Well… friendly… polite… charming. Um, a real charmer. And a groover, to use a word of the time! Used to go to festivals and stuff. Isle of Wight. That sort of thing. A weekend hippy, they used to be called... I never actually went out with him. More's the pity!' She gave a self-deprecating chuckle. 'Not his type, I guess. But he did knock around for a while with one of the other librarians who told me that he was quite a name in the counter-culture and that he used to write for the *International Times*. She said he was full of great stories about it all.'

'So what do you think made him want to become a librarian?'

'I'm not sure. He read like billy-o. And I think he liked the life of the library. I don't know what, the order, perhaps. He was always very helpful to me, carrying piles of books, learning where to return them to according to the Dewey system. In fact it was when he was helping me one day that he asked me how I had become a librarian... he wished he was one. And that was the moment it all started. I told him that if he got a job in the library... There were plenty going at that time. The public library service was expanding like billy-o then. Not like now, when they can't close branches fast enough, sadly. Scandalous... I asked if he had a degree and he said no, so—'

'Said he had no degree?'

'That's what he said.'

'Really? I thought he had a degree from Columbia University, in America.'

Molly looked puzzled. 'Not that I am aware of... In fact, I'm pretty sure he didn't have a degree. He said he'd left school at fifteen. Always regretted not taking his education further... That's why he spent so long in the library – trying to make up for what he'd missed... Anyway, I told him that if he became a library assistant he could get qualified on the job by the Library Association. And that's what he did.'

I was puzzled by this. But intrigued, of course. 'What job did Carlo have before he became a librarian?'

'He worked in a record shop – I think it might have been in the arcade off Coldharbour Lane… And before that…' Molly looked pensive for a moment, her ebullience checked. 'I remember him telling me once that he had been a milkman before that, somewhere round Streatham way. He'd given it up, he said, because one day, early in the morning, he'd stumbled upon a terrible beating-up – a gang of young men battering someone with baseball bats. Or coshes, I can't remember which… I don't know why he told me. It obviously distressed him to remember it, and he was shaking the whole time he was telling me. And for a while afterwards.'

'How awful… So he decided to work indoors. Got a job in the record shop… But he gave that up and came to work in the library here… And got his qualification?'

A nod from Molly, a smile restored to her face. 'He did. And he worked very hard. Was very good. And he would still spend hours here even when he wasn't working. Still reading like billy-o… But I'll tell you something funny… Well, it made me laugh. When he started work with us, he had to rein back with the clothes. No more Mr Male Mannequin! Miss Butchart, the senior librarian – Miss Whiplash we used to call her behind her back!' Molly let out a gleeful squawk that attracted a few eyes towards us. 'Miss Whiplash was very strict, an absolute stickler, and she wanted Carlo to dress normally – jacket and tie, sober colours. Well, I worried about this… he could be a bit excitable sometimes, you know, sort of manic in a way… But he was an absolute sweetie! He looked so cute when he first came in like that… a little self-conscious, I guess, but so proud to be doing what he should to fit in.' She chuckled. 'But there was one concession he didn't make – his shoes! He still wore these wonderful Chelsea boots with Cuban heels and pointy toes! Very à la mode!' Another peal of laughter.

'And he moved on in 1970?'

'Yes, I guess it was about then. He wanted to become a university librarian. I always thought there was a kind of restlessness to him… a kind of urgency to be moving on.' She mused for a moment. 'Anyway, he wanted to move on. He was a bright man and a very quick learner, and I think he wanted to work in an environment that was more academic… I suppose he found dear old Brixton a little limiting. So he applied to a few unis and eventually got a job somewhere on the south coast. I forget where.'

*

Carlo's university was a modern campus with many shiny new buildings, all steel and glass and coloured panels in the modern idiom. I was sitting in a small room in the HR department, going through his employment record, a hefty file of his thirty years of service. I had asked Luca to arrange permission for me to access the file, knowing that, data protection laws being what they were these days, I would get nowhere without such authority.

There were two references from the library, one from the stern stickler Miss Whiplash, as Molly had called her. It was glowing in its praise of Carlo's work ethic, his helpfulness to borrowers, his breadth of knowledge in all kinds of areas. The letter of application, a copy of which I had already seen, was there and also, of course, a CV. Carlo had recorded his place of birth as Trieste, year 1935. There were no details of his schooling, only his university degree: a BA in Liberal Arts taken in 1956. The other qualification he recorded was his librarian's certification. His employment prior to his post at Brixton Library was recorded simply as 'Various'.

It was a staggeringly brief CV. But as I looked through the rest of the file I saw that he had quickly established himself at the Institute, its status when he started. And it was clear that he and his work grew quickly in stature, just as the institute did, finally becoming a university. In the later stages of his career there were appraisals, all of them glowing and most of them containing what would seem to be merely token 'targets for further development'.

I asked if I could see the head of HR. I wanted to know whether qualifications were always checked. Always, these days, she said. In the past? Not always, but often. I wondered if there was any way of knowing. There wasn't.

When I asked if any of his former colleagues were still teaching at the university she named two, picked up the phone, established that one of them, Phil Carpenter, was free at the moment, and happy to have a brief chat. When he arrived we were taken to the same small room in which I had read Carlo's file.

Phil spoke with great warmth about Carlo and about Brenda, saying what a good couple they made, how everyone at the university was so pleased for them when they got together, and how utterly cruel it was that she was taken away from him so young. And left him with the little children to look after. Carlo had notably good relationships with staff and was wonderfully generous with students, giving them all the time and help he felt they needed. 'He always struck me,' Phil said, 'as someone who took great pleasure in the learning process. He himself embodied perfectly the notion of life-long learning, was always adding to his great store of knowledge, never lost his curiosity. And he took the greatest of pleasure in nurturing students in whom he saw that same thirst for learning.'

*

When I got home that evening I did a Google search to find out how I could access Columbia University graduation rolls. It was easy enough, all online, a complete list of the annual registers digitised and available, no login required. All I had to do was look in the 'Catalogue Number for the sessions of 1954–1955'. To be certain of missing nothing, I looked at the student registers for the years either side of this. There was no trace of any d'Abruzzi; none of C. Adams, which according to Theresa, was the other name by which he might have gone.

It was mysterious and disturbing. But then it merely confirmed what Molly Dibben had told me: that Carlo had said that he had no formal education beyond the age of fifteen. The mystery only deepened when I decided to research his family tree a little more closely: to flesh out the bones of that charming piece of work that he had drawn up in his childish handwriting, with the royal Carlo, a stick man wearing a wonky crown, appearing at the base of the family tree.

I soon realised how very confusing Carlo's supposed lineage was, and it seemed that he was both the source and the victim of the muddle. When he claimed, as he did on the recordings Theresa had made of him, that his father was Umberto and his mother Maria, he was perhaps thinking of King Victor Emmanuel III's heir, Umberto II, who, for a mere month in 1946, had been King of Italy before it became a republic. There were four children to the marriage, all of them still alive. None of them, clearly, Carlo.

According to the family tree he'd drawn as a child, Carlo's grandfather had been Prince Umberto, Count of Salemi. And yet when I looked this man up on Wikipedia I discovered the following: 'Umberto died a month before the end of the war. The official court bulletin recorded that he was killed in action, but in fact he died of the Spanish flu.' He had died in 1918, without issue.

*

The face that greeted me as Theresa opened the door was unduly pale and stretched tight in a mask of grief and tiredness. She had told me on the phone that things at work were exhaustingly busy. Like all GP practices in London, everywhere in the country perhaps, hers was being massively overstretched and chronically under-funded. When she showed me into the sitting room, I noticed that it was uncharacteristically messy, looking as though it had not seen a hoover or duster for a while. An untidy pile of newspapers lay discarded on the floor.

I had rung her in the morning to say I wanted to see her. Fine, she said, she would knock up a simple meal for us. In the event, she ordered pizzas when I arrived, apologising for not having the energy to cook.

Because it was she who had commissioned me for the project about her father, I felt bound to tell her about my recent discoveries, even before discussing it with Luca. So, as we waited for the food to arrive, sipping wine together, I told her about the trip to Brixton. It was, of course, a challenge I had worried about on the journey to Hammersmith, agonising about the best way to tell her what I had discovered: about the conundrums and contradictions of this man her father, a charming, learned man, much loved, much admired, who appeared to have lied about his lineage and about his education; who appeared to have lied his way into a job in which he would be happily successful for three decades.

The pizzas arrived and, as we began to eat them, she asked me what I had found out from the Brixton Library.

'Well,' I said, 'I met this lovely old biddy – Molly – who had worked with your father. She was very fond of him… and would have loved him to have asked her out, I suspect! She said that he worked in a record shop in Brixton, but used to spend hours in the library, reading prolifically – "like billy-o" was how Molly put it. He wanted to become a librarian and found out from Molly that he could learn on the job and get certification from the Library Association.'

Theresa was listening with interest, too tired to smile perhaps, but smiling inwardly, I suspected.

'The thing is, Theresa, that your dad apparently told Molly that he had no formal education after the age of fifteen, had no degree.'

There was a moment's silence and then, 'But that's nonsense. You know it's nonsense, Nick.' Her eyes had quickly become energised with a spark of anger. 'He had a degree from Columbia.'

As gently as I could, I said, 'I don't think he did. I really don't think he did.'

'Of course he bloody did. What are you trying to say?' She banged her pizza down on the table, so roughly that it nearly bounced out of its box.

'Theresa... Theresa... I've checked the old Columbia records, student records, graduation records. The name d'Abruzzi doesn't—'

'Adams. Charlie Adams.' She shouts this. The body that had appeared so weighted with exhaustion when I had arrived was now mobile, electric.

'No... I checked that too.'

'Look, this Polly, Molly, whatever, she doesn't know what she's talking about. Papa was probably playing games with her.' The anger-filled face, the raised voice, both now had a touch of desperation in them.

'...There's something else... That sweet family tree that your father wrote out when he was a child... it can't be right. He said that his grandfather was Prince Umberto. That can't be. Umberto died in 1918 of the Spanish flu. He never got married. Never had children.'

'Rubbish, rubbish, rubbish!' She was screaming now. 'It's you and your nasty poking about. Sticking your nose where it's not wanted.'

'Theresa, I'm just researching your father's life, as you asked me to.'

'I didn't ask you to nose around in Brixton or look up his family tree. It's none of your bloody business.' Her eyes had taken on a manic look. 'Get out! GET OUT! I'm sick of you poking about. Jumping into my knickers and prying into my family.'

I couldn't believe what I was hearing. It was beyond absurd. It seemed that a wall of unreason had descended, immuring Theresa.

'Look, Theresa—'

She grabbed the pizza box and banged it down hard on my head, the pizza jumping out and disintegrating on my shoulders, my feet, the floor. 'Get out of my house, you lying little toad.'

And I did. As quickly as I could.

14

'Nichol-arse, me old son! Guess what!'

I hadn't spoken to George since his intrusion into Carlo's funeral and I was disinclined to speak to him now on the phone. So I replied with an unenthusiastic 'What?'

'I've done me photoshoot! The photoshoot you suggested. Boats! On the Thames!' George was sounding his irrepressible old self. Was there any other way he ever sounded?

'Great,' I said flatly.

'So. Yer going come and see 'em?'

'George, I was pretty disgusted with the way you crashed Carlo d'Abruzzi's funeral. I couldn't believe it when I saw you lurking in the bushes.'

'Well, listen, mate, I'm sorry. Yeah, I'm sorry. But… well. Needs must. I thought there might be some nobs at the funeral, what with Charlo being a big cheese and all. I gotta earn a crust. Just like you… Now, are you going to come over and see the pics or not?'

As George said, I had to earn a crust.

*

The Papararium, as George jokingly called his attractive Chiswick house, had a small carefully tended front garden, a neatness that was mirrored in his well-organised kitchen-living room; both contrasted with the mess of his office upstairs, where I was now standing, gazing out of the window onto the small garden. There was a contradiction between the tidiness of George's living space and the relative chaos of his work space; I wondered whether this reflected the tension between his roguish paparazzi pursuits and his current desire for something more respectable, something purer, something which could take him back, perhaps, to the days of his earliest celebrity shot, which had captured the wholesome, girl-next-doorness of Kate Winslet.

In the garden below, a robin was attached to a hanging bird feeder, stocking up for its next burst of energetic singing.

'Do you get many birds coming to the feeders, George?'

'Yeah. Fair number. Not as many species as in Reading when I was a kid. But plenty...'

George had certainly been busy on his photoshoot, and his project had ranged over a much longer stretch of the Thames than I had suggested in the first draft of my article about him. He had helpfully printed out the photos for me. They were strikingly good. Unsurprisingly, he knew exactly how to use light to its best effect – important, I imagined, when working with water. And he was also very good at composition. I had assumed that this was not something a paparazzo normally had much time for, in the haste to capture the fleeting shot of a moving celebrity.

The collection fell into two groupings: leisure craft and houseboats. The first set started with an elderly couple sitting in the cuddy of a small day boat. A wicker picnic basket is sitting on a small table and they are cheerfully toasting the camera. In other photos they are feeding the ducks, they are mooring the boat, they are in an emptying lock, the shining green algae stretching up above them. Always there is a contented look on their faces.

Another series was of a twenty-three-foot narrow-beam cruiser. Aboard a young family, all looking healthily tanned from the summer sun and its river-reflected rays. The parents are smiling proudly and joyfully; a little girl of about seven is grinning self-consciously and her younger brother is looking awkwardly at the camera. There is a more relaxed shot of the family going through a lock, the little girl holding one of the ropes, her mother the other, the little boy sitting on a step absorbed in the busy action of the rising boats.

Ahead of this cruiser, in the same lock, is a gin palace, huge and gleaming, lording it over the smaller craft. The luxurious interiors are shown in their vulgar glory, as are the people aboard: three bronzed women, expensively dressed in recreational summer clothing, two men. All have glasses in their hands. One of the men is wearing a white captain's uniform, the gold-braided peak of his cap indicating his place in the hierarchy of the crew: captain of the ship, or at least pretend skipper for the day.

The houseboat series started in London aboard a huge vessel moored in an expensive marina. The interior is expansive and plush and, save for the different-shaped windows, might just as well have been the interior of any apartment in any of the numerous newly built blocks surrounding the basin. Significantly, perhaps, no people appear in any of the shots of this boat, chiming with the impersonal nature of it all.

The next series was of a traditional, elegantly curving Dutch barge lived in by a professional couple who worked in the city. The furnishings are quirky and are all in apple-pie order; or ship-shape and in Bristol fashion, perhaps.

In the outer London area, beyond Kingston, a long shot shows a large gathering of houseboats. George has focused on one very basic dwelling which seems to be little more than a mobile home mounted on a pontoon; but clearly it is loved, with its fresh, cheerful blue paint, its pot plants and its trellises with well-tended climbers. Close by there is another, much larger home, similarly mounted on a floating platform, but three storeys high, clad in larch. Visually, this is an interesting boat. It has an irregular roofline and each storey has a different-shaped balcony; the smaller top floor opens out onto a roof terrace.

George had clearly been engaged by this collection of houseboats. He had captured an evening gathering on the eyot that seemed to be the focal point of this community. There is something very English in the scene. It is partly the clothing, partly the rather goofy expressions on the faces of some of the people and partly the presence of the obligatory barbecue.

Perhaps the most interesting photos were of a small, scruffy little boat, by the look of it moored much further upstream. It is narrow and probably no more than twenty feet long, consisting of a hotchpotch of cabin space built to different heights and from different materials – wood,

GRP, metal. Inside, there are essentially two small spaces, one for living and one for sleeping. George had taken some moody photos of the interior, dark, with the odd shaft of light catching a rudimentary piece of furnishing. Sitting on a tiny, battered armchair is a wiry, bearded man, staring into the camera with a gaze of wise contentment. Another photo, posed presumably, is of the man hunched up on a small bunk bed feigning sleep. Another shows him on the river bank, cooking over a camping stove.

It was a fine collection. George had created interest in his themes, the contrast between the use of the river for living and for leisure, and the disparity between rich and poor. But more striking was the photography itself. Seeing how skilfully George manipulated light and shade, how intuitively he seemed to beam onto a tiny detail of interest, made me feel that he was wasted as a paparazzo. I was convinced that he was making absolutely the right decision in deciding to move into photojournalism.

'You've got some excellent pictures here, George… Now, as I envisage the article, it would be about you writing the story so that you get to the point of taking this collection rather than majoring on the collection itself. Is that how you see it?'

'Yeah. Sort of. I mean, the pics will need some sort of explanation, won't they?'

'Well, yes, captions, certainly… Did you take any notes?'

George shuffled around in a drawer and brought out a few scruffy sheets of paper. In a surprisingly neat hand, but hardly punctuated at all and with the spelling all over the place, he had noted names, places, and miscellaneous comments.

'That's great, George. What we need to do is make a selection and then for me to write a paragraph or two as to exactly what you were trying to achieve with this collection. And add that to a revised version of what I sent to you a few weeks ago.'

'Spot on, mate.' George hesitated. 'What is important, though, is that it sounds something like me. I don't want to come across as a pretentious twat, see what I mean? It's gotta be me. My voice.'

And he wasn't kidding. He was insistent, this lurker in the bushes, this sniper snapping from unseen hidey-holes. He wanted the article to contain the authentic voice and identity of George Nelson. He did not want a disconnect between the roguish paparazzo and the respectable photojournalist that he hoped to become. He wanted them to be of a piece with each other – at peace with each other, perhaps – so that there was a single, indivisible identity of the two personae.

'Of course, George, of course.'

'You're a good'un, Nick... And I'm sorry I got yer gander up at the funeral. Shouldn't have done it... Mind you, no one of interest there, anyway. Apart from the geezer in the bushes—'

'You, you mean—'

'Nah, not me, guv, the relative chap. Least, I assume he was a relative. Looked like he was.'

'George, I don't know what you are talking about.'

'Well, I know that I was hid behind the tree. But there was this other bloke hanging back, lurking just out of sight so he couldn't be seen by the funeral party. And he looked the spit of Charlo. Only younger.'

'You mean Carlo's son – Luca?'

'No. Older. Fifties, I'd guess.'

'When you say spit of Carlo, had you ever seen him – Carlo?'

'Nah. But I saw the pic of him in *The Times* – with the bit you wrote. The pic at the Albert Hall…And this bloke at the funeral looked like what I imagined Charlie would of grown into.'

'It's Carlo, George—'

'Carlo. Charlo. Charlie. Charlie Farley. Whatever… Look, I'll show you some pics of him if you like. Hang on. I'll just print 'em off.'

He moved to the computer. I peered over his shoulder as he located a file incongruously named 'Fun.'.

'Fun?'

'Funeral. Charlie Farley's funeral. Old matey what was buried.'

The earlier images he brought up in the file were of Theresa. In some of the shots she looked achingly beautiful as she stood by the graveside; in others, once her grief had broken her composure, her face was disfigured by the ugly distortions of her hysteria. And then we came on to the mysterious interloper and I saw immediately that the man in shot had to be a relative of Carlo's. The similarity was astonishing. The hair, the profile with its distinctive Roman nose, the eyes.

I made my way through the printouts slowly. None of them had been taken head on; George's position, under the cover of his yew tree, had given him a view at an angle of about forty-five degrees. The man wasn't exactly hiding in the bushes, as George had originally said, but he was ensuring that he remained away from the funeral group and largely beyond their view. He was dressed in a dark suit and was wearing a plain maroon tie. The posture of this mysterious man was interesting. His hands were held together loosely in front of him, half in prayer it seemed, and his head was slightly bowed: though physically apart from the burial party, he clearly was emotionally a part of it. I was sure that he was offering his respects to Carlo.

'I don't know what to say, George. As far as I know, the only blood relatives that Carlo had in this country were his two children. And I wouldn't begin to know what to do with this information. As far as Carlo's children are concerned, there are no uncles or cousins. Carlo was a single child… And of course there is no way of tracking this chap down.'

George tapped his nose conspiratorially. 'Let me show you something, mate.'

He went back to the desk and reopened the 'Fun.' folder. The images he was now clicking on were of cars, more specifically their registration plates. He pointed to a fat leather notebook on the table. 'That's my passport to wealth and 'appiness, Nick me old son. My file of the fantastic and the famous! Names, addresses, associates, partners – legit or "behind the scenes" …And car registration numbers. Always have it with me. And at an event I will usually snap the cars so that I can check if there are any celebs there… And there weren't!' He pulls a mock-tragic face.

'I don't see how this helps me, George.'

'Ah!' He taps the side of his nose again and says, 'You may think I'm a bit of a reprobate, Nick. Or a lot of a reprobate, perhaps. And perhaps I am. But I have my uses… And I have my contacts. I've got a tame plod at the Met – I won't go into how I tamed him for the moment! – and if I give him this list of reg numbers, he will give me a list of names and addresses… A tidy little arrangement, don't you think?'

'Erm… well… I guess.' I felt grubby just having the conversation. On the other hand, finding out the identity of this mystery man surely was imperative. '…Okay, George, you do that… though I don't know what kind of sense I'll make of it all.'

*

That evening I rang Luca. I didn't tell him about the mystery man at the funeral, but I filled him in on my findings from Brixton Library, the university, and the childless Prince Umberto. He did not express huge surprise and did not seem unduly upset. I also told him about my visit to Theresa and the crazy way it had ended. He apologised on her behalf. But I should understand, he said, how overwhelmingly grief-stricken she was at losing her father, how that was intensified by the way that it had happened. And it was not a good time – an impossible time, in fact – for her to have to confront these additional shocks. I could understand that. Poor Theresa had been doubly bereaved. She had lost her father and then lost the man she thought he was. Luca and I left it that I would deal only with him for the time being.

As soon as I put down the phone it rang again. It was George. 'Nickolai! I'm banging over an email with the names and addresses of the car owners at the funeral!'

15

As I drove towards Angelo Goretti's house in Watford, I speculated on how our meeting might go, and was quietly optimistic. Angelo Goretti, I had discovered, was the name of the Carlo-Luca look-alike. He it was who had stood unobtrusively on the periphery of Carlo's funeral.

The list of names and addresses that George had emailed to me had not presented any real challenges of guesswork. There was only one Italian-sounding name. Of course, it might have been fortuitous and a false lead, but I took a chance on this being the name of the mystery presence. His number was in the phone book. When I called the man, I was slightly fearful that he would take offence at my inquisitiveness, my intrusion.

'Mr Goretti? Angelo Goretti?'

'Yes. Who is this?' The accent had just a residual trace of Italian to it; the voice was neither defensive nor aggressive, merely matter-of-fact curious.

I told him that I was a friend of the d'Abruzzi family. I said I hoped that he would not find it amiss if I asked whether he had attended Carlo's funeral in Wimborne.

There was a silence for a moment. And now there was an element of defensiveness in the tone of voice. 'Erm… Yes… Yes, I was there… Is there a problem?'

'No, no, not at all. Look, it's probably best if we talk about this face-to-face rather than over the phone. The thing is, I am researching the life of Carlo d'Abruzzi… I couldn't help noticing your strong resemblance to him—'

'Ah. I was trying not to be seen. How did you trace me, by the way?'

I really didn't want to go into that at this stage. I still felt grubby from the help that George had given me. 'Look, I am going to make the assumption that you are related to Carlo in some way and that that was the reason you went to his funeral. And I am also going to make the assumption, unless you expressly tell me that this is not what you want… I'm going to make the assumption that we would both benefit from meeting up and talking this through.'

He told me that he was Carlo's nephew, the son of Carlo's elder brother Alfonso, and that he had never met Carlo, whom his father had said was long dead. He agreed that it would be good to talk the whole story through, exchanging our different pieces of the tale. So we arranged to meet the following Saturday morning, at his house in Watford.

The route I was taking was via the M4 and M25, longer in mileage but quicker in time. And more wasteful in energy, as I should have realised before I set off: the north-western arc of the M25 is one of the most irritating pieces of roadway in the entire country. As I moved from lane to lane long along a stretch of motorway that had the gall to call itself 'smart', I wondered where Angelo would fit into

Carlo's backstory. I had not mentioned him to either Luca or Theresa. In fact I had not spoken to Theresa at all since her wild, irrational rant. But at least for my peace of mind, if not for hers, I wanted to get the story of Carlo straight.

*

Angelo welcomed me warmly. His wife, he told me, was out shopping, but would be back later in the morning. He was taller than he appeared in George's photos, but his resemblance to Carlo was even more striking. And he had – I hadn't really noticed this on the phone – that same rich baritone voice that Carlo had and which lived on in Luca.

He took me into the sitting room and offered me a coffee. We exchanged some small talk and then he said, 'But of course it's Carlo you're here for… You know, it's so strange meeting someone who actually knew Carlo.'

'Well, not really. A little. And only very recently. I had been commissioned by his children, Theresa and Luca—'

'His children, yes. The two who led the funeral procession. They looked young enough to be his grandchildren, but then I reread the obituary when I got home and saw they were born in 1990.'

'Yes. Carlo and his wife Brenda had their family late – a late windfall. So… they, Theresa initially, wanted me to write the biography of Carlo—'

'Of course. He was famous—'

'Ah. No. Not really—'

'But the obituary—'

'Hmm. I think we better begin at the beginning!'

'Okay… Fire away.'

'So, when Theresa came to me she was under the impression that her father, that Carlo, had been a famous figure, highly influential in the 1960s… which turns out not to be strictly true.'

'Good heavens!'

'And she also believed that he was descended from Victor Emmanuel II on his father's side and had a Bonaparte pedigree on his mother's side. Which also turns out not to be true.'

'Well, no, I knew that that bit of the obituary wasn't true. Carlo d'Abruzzi was actually Carlo Goretti and his grandfather was a shop owner from Ljubljana.'

At that moment there was a rattling of the front door and Helen, Angelo's wife, arrived in the hallway with three bags of shopping. Angelo sprang up, saying, 'Excuse me a moment,' and rushed to carry them into the kitchen for her. He then introduced me to her. She was a striking woman, elegantly dressed, I thought, for someone returning from a weekend household shopping trip. She had dark, direct eyes, black mid-length hair carefully styled, and came towards me with a natural grace of movement.

'Ah, Mr Barry. Angelo was intrigued when he got your call. And so excited. For years he had assumed that his uncle was dead, long dead, and then one day – by chance, one might say, but then he always reads *The Times* obituaries – he came rushing to me, waving the paper at me. "Look! Look!" he said. "Look at this photo!" I was staggered! "That's you when you were younger!" I said, although the hair was bit long and he seemed to be smoking a joint! "This chap is called Carlo, Helen. And he was born in 1935 in Trieste! It's Uncle Carlo. It's got to be!"'

While Helen prepared some lunch, Angelo continued his account of his and Carlo's ancestors.

'Although I have an Italian name, I come from Slovene stock originally. My great-grandfather grew up in Ljubljana, which at the time was a Slav-speaking part of the Austrian empire. He was called Viktor Gregorič. He owned a leather shop and did quite well for himself, but in the final years of the nineteenth century, things – the economy – were not doing well. The last straw was when his house was destroyed in an earthquake in 1895. So he decided to move to Trieste, which at the time was the great, thriving seaport of the Austrian Empire. And he set up a shoe shop there, and was doing very well in no time at all. Sadly Viktor died prematurely in 1920, and his son – my grandfather Boŝko, Boŝko Gregorič, only nineteen at the time – took over the shop. And he did really well and was quickly able to expand the business. But it was just at that time when things were changing. Do you know anything about the history of that part of the world, Nick?'

I shook my head.

'No? Okay. So let me give you a quick history lesson.' I nodded. 'I'll try to make it simple and brief… Well, as part of the carve-up of Europe following the First World War, the Austrian Littoral, which included Trieste, passed into the hands of Italy. Not a bad thing in itself – Trieste had always been a melting pot of nationalities. But Italy was a young country, recently unified, and it was strongly nationalistic, and once the Fascists got into power things changed for the worse really quickly. In the early nineteen twenties anti-Slavic policies started being enforced. These included the Italianisation programme, which required – forced – Slovenians and Croats to Italianise their names. My grandfather now spelt his first name in the Italian way, Bosco. My grandmother Mare become Maria. And the surname was changed from Gregorič to Goretti. In different circumstances, my father would have been called Alfonz rather than Alfonso and Carlo would have been called Karel.'

'Gosh. How extraordinary!'

'Well. Not really… Anyway, it gets worse. By 1925 Mussolini had already established his dictatorship and of course it was in his interests to bolster a sense of national identity and to stoke the fires of hatred against "the other". The Slovenes in Trieste tended to be middle class and well-to-do. The Italians in the city – and their numbers had swelled hugely after the war – were mostly working class or lower middle class. They hated the Slovenes. They began attacking Slovene-owned shops, businesses, legal firms – just as the Nazis would do to the Jews in Germany a little later. My grandfather's shop was attacked several times, but never destroyed.'

'What age was your father, at this stage, Angelo?'

'He was born in 1930. He was five years older than Carlo… Anyway, while many Slovene families fled Trieste to what was then Yugoslavia, my grandfather was determined to stay put. But he made a big mistake. He had become outraged by what was happening to his people. And he started floating around on the fringes of a Slovene anti-fascist organisation, TIGR, a group of militant activists. In 1930, the year my father was born – my grandfather was not yet involved with TIGR – the group carried out several bomb attacks in the city, targeting military and government premises. There was a trial, there were executions, but the group quickly resurfaced. It was mainly young people – I don't really know why my grandfather got involved. He had a young family to look after.'

Angelo paused. Naturally it upset him to talk about these things. But he knew he needed to tell me, so he continued. 'It was April, 1940. My father, Alfonso, was off school for the day, I don't why, at home in the apartment with his mother. Carlo, five years old, had gone out with his nanny, Rosa. Suddenly there was frantic banging on the door. One of the shop staff was screaming.'

What Angelo told me that morning – haltingly, struggling to get the words out, at times compressing his lips to prevent himself weeping – was profoundly shocking.

I was moved by his story. By its details and by the intensity of his feelings. 'Thank you, Angelo, for sharing that with me. It is very good of you.'

He smiled at me, a genuinely warm smile, if still tinged with some of the sadness of his story. 'That's all right, Nick. I'm happy to share it. With the eventual emergence of Carlo, it makes the story more complete.'

'And your father stayed in Trieste?'

'Yes. He got a job in the docks and then, when his mother, Maria, received government compensation for the shoe shop, they set up a small grocery store together. He got married in the mid-fifties to Giulia, my mother. And then in 1959 I came along and a couple of years later Carla, my sister. Named after her uncle!'

*

Over lunch I asked him about his move to England. He had trained in Trieste as a tree surgeon. He'd wanted to work in England for a year or two to learn English, came over in 1981, and would have returned to Italy eventually, where his parents had remained.

'But I met Helen!' He reached across the table and put his hand over hers.

'Lucky me!' She beamed.

'And lucky me!'

After getting married and before starting a family, he had gone to college as a mature student to get a qualification in town and country planning. He had finally ended up as a tree officer in the Watford Planning Department.

As Helen was peeling some fruit she'd brought in for pudding, she said, 'It's a strange thing, names, aren't they? I would have been Helen Gregorič if Angelo's grandfather hadn't been made to Italianise his name. And do you know, our son, David, when he was at university decided to change his name by deed poll, to anglicise it… to Gregory! David Gregory, which I guess is closer to his great-grandfather's name than Goretti!'

'And I wonder where d'Abruzzi comes in,' Angelo wondered.

'Actually I can tell you. As part of my researches I looked closely at the family tree of the Italian monarchy and found there was a branch somewhere along the line of d'Abruzzis. I guess Carlo opted for that when he was searching for an identity.'

'Hmm. That's all very odd, isn't it?' said Helen.

'So where are you going to take your researches from here, Nick?'

'I'm not sure, Angelo. I would like to trace Carlo's journey to England and find out about his childhood. He talked about growing up on a farm in Devon, but so much of what he said was unreliable, so I just don't know... You don't have any clues, do you?'

He shook his head. 'None. I had long thought him dead until I read the obituary in *The Times*... With all its inaccuracies! I wonder where the information came from.'

I longed to hide behind the anonymity of the absent by-line. But Angelo had been so open, his wife so welcoming, that I thought I had to be honest. 'From me, Angelo. I wrote that piece. From information that Carlo and Theresa had given me.'

'Oh.' And Angelo quickly moved on. 'Do Angelo's children, Theresa and... Luca, did you say, go by the name d'Abruzzi?'

I nodded. And then I asked Angelo why he had not made himself known at the funeral or the burial.

'Well, I was too late for the funeral service. And the burial... I felt it wasn't the right time. But I really do think I should introduce myself... to my cousins. My newly discovered cousins!'

Helen nodded vigorously. 'Oh, yes, darling. You would so love that. To think you have relatives in England! And they would love it, too, I'm sure.'

I thought back to the cassette tapes, to the part where Theresa had asked – with longing, I felt – why she had no uncles or aunts or cousins, and of the deep pain I sensed in Carlo's response.

'I think it would be good, too,' I said, 'but first let me ask you a favour. Give me a little time to see if I can find out more about Carlo's early years before we spring this shock on them. This delightful shock.'

*

When I got home I went through the day's correspondence. Although the fuss about my piece in *The Times* had long since abated, there was a belated email on the matter, forwarded by Robert Wainwright, the obituaries editor:

> I read with interest your obituary on Carlo d'Abruzzi (5th June) and the subsequent letters and corrections. I knew the man briefly (he was then calling himself Charlie) in the mid-1960s. We used to go to the pub together occasionally and to the odd gig, the most truly memorable of which was the Poetry Incarnation at the Albert Hall in 1965. We sat next to each other at that notable event, and I will never forget the extraordinary and intense excitement Carlo/Charlie displayed throughout the evening – something I thought at the time was verging on the hysterical. As far as I can recall, we both smoked some marijuana, but in his case this seemed to heighten rather than mellow a mood that can only be described as manic. There appeared to be something almost unhinged in his demeanour.
>
> The main focus of his excitement that evening was Allen Ginsberg – 'this great man', he kept calling him. This great man, he said, had broken the mould. Here was a poet who was famous the world over, a poet, not film star or a singer, a poet who

shared celebrity status with the likes of Bob Dylan and John Lennon. A celebrity poet! He couldn't get over it. And during Ginsberg's recital he was frequently scribbling notes in a jotter pad he had brought with him. Two quotations in particular come back to me (I have checked the accuracy by listening once more to Ginsberg's recital, which can be found online). 'Come sweetly / back to my Self as I was.' And 'I am a mass of sores and worms / I am false Name the prey / of Yamantaka Devourer of / Strange dreams.'

When we met a few times subsequently, he would repeat a version of these lines, which he had conflated – either because he misremembered them or, more likely, because he had reworked them into something more meaningful for himself. 'I am false name, devourer of strange dreams. / Come sweetly back to myself as I was.' I think I am quoting him accurately. He repeated the lines several times to me – incanted them, rather – as though they had become some kind of a mantra for him.

We drifted apart later that year and I had quite forgotten about him until I read his obituary and saw the photo of us both together at the Albert Hall. What has prompted me to write is that I wonder whether he didn't undergo some important psychic experience that night which might explain his subsequent 'inventions' and his enormously inflated claims to have been a man of some influence in that momentous decade.

He was an agreeable man and I did enjoy our brief acquaintance, but I did sense a fragility in him and I wondered – or certainly have wondered since reading the obituary – whether he had mental health issues.

Kind regards,
John Williamson

16

The Gazette is subtitled 'The Official Public Record' and is an invaluable online resource. I had returned from my visit to the Gorettis knowing Carlo's birth name and keen to explore his name change. Prompted by Helen's revelation that her son, David, had changed his name by deed poll, I was now looking for another transformation of the Goretti name.

It was George who had tipped me the wink and told me to look in *The Gazette*. George naturally knew all the wheezes and dodges for uncovering people's past identities. Apparently, these uncovered little snippets of information could sometimes provide useful leverage when dealing directly with celebrities. He told me with some pride and some delight that he was the first person to discover – by looking in *The London Gazette*, as *The Gazette* then was – that a well-known and much-loved television presenter was christened and grew up as Dennis Smellie. "Den is smelly! Geddit?' he said in his characteristic over-kill of what he deemed to be his priceless wit. According to George, Carlo's name change would almost certainly have been registered.

My first search was for Carlo Goretti. It revealed nothing. I then searched for Carlo d'Abruzzi. Bingo!

> Notice is hereby given that by a Deed Poll dated 24th August 1965, and enrolled in the Supreme Court of Judicature on 29th September 1965, I, CARLO VICTOR D'ABRUZZI of 21 Alder Crescent, Herne Hill, a citizen of the United Kingdom and Colonies by naturalisation, have abandoned the name of Charles Abbott. —Dated this 4th day of October 1965. Carlo d'Abruzzi, formerly Charles Abbott.

Charlie Abbott, not Charlie Adams, his alter ego, according to Theresa. Another inaccuracy – or an invention of Carlo's, perhaps – might be the names of Carlo's foster parents, Dora and Leonard. Supposedly they had taken him in and brought him up on their farm in Devon. On the other hand, what if these names were neither inaccurate nor invented? If Carlo had indeed been adopted by Dora and Leonard Abbott?

How could I find out whether these people had owned or lived on a farm in Devon in the 1940s? And if they did, whether their descendants still owned the farm? I was quickly on the phone to my go-to man of the moment, George.

'Well, the first thing to do, mate, is to look at the 1939 Register. Known as *The Wartime Domesday Book*. Well, by some. It's the only record of the British population between 1921 and 1951.'

'How come?' I asked.

'The 1931 census was destroyed in the war and the 1941 one never happened. For obvious reasons. So, the 1939

Register is the only place to look. Fortunately it has very recently gone online. And if you find the name of the farm, you can look up a recent electoral register and see who lives there now.' George was sounding more like a librarian or someone from the Citizens' Advice Bureau than a rough diamond paparazzo. I had always had my suspicions that the George beneath the cockney geezer persona was the studious, serious-minded boy his mother had brought up in Reading.

No sooner had that thought struck me than George became the diamond geezer once more. 'Listen, me old son, you bin good to me and one good turn deserves anuvver. Give me the details and I'll do the necessaries... It can come out of me payment to you for yer story on me!' I could almost hear his grin coming down the line.

*

It was an excited George who reported back to me.

'Do you want the good news or the bad news first, sunshine?' he asked.

'The good news, of course!'

'Righty-ho. So. A Leonard and Dora Abbott did indeed have a farm in west Devon in the war years. Highfold Farm, Stowford. I've looked on the map, mate. It's north of Okehampton, a couple of miles off the A30.'

'Thank you, George! What a star you are!'

'I thenk you, I thenk you.' I imagined him doing a little bow as he said this. 'And, er, the bad news?'

'Oh gosh, yes, there was some bad news—'

'The farm does not appear to be in the same family.

Disappointing, I know. It's now owned by a Mike and Rosie Barlow.'

*

Lunch would be waiting for me at Highfold Farm where I was heading to meet the Barlows.

I had rung the farm shortly after George's call. It was Mike who had answered. I told him that I was researching the farm's war-time years when it was owned by Dora and Leonard Abbott. 'Tell me,' I said, 'would you happen to know when the Abbott family sold up?'

'They didn't,' he replied. 'I married Rosie Abbott, granddaughter of Leonard and Dora.'

My heart had skipped a beat. '...So Rosie was an Abbott?'

'Yes, her father was John Abbot. We took over the farm when he died in 2003.'

I told him I would love to talk to his wife. He called her to the phone and I explained my mission. She had heard of Carlo, she said. And yes, of course, I must come down and talk to her. It was a long drive, so I should stay the night. It would give us longer to talk. She sounded welcoming and warm, and very keen to be helpful.

*

As soon she heard the car approaching Rosie came into the drive to greet me, accompanied by two sheep dogs appearing from different directions, intent on checking me out. She was of what you might call a sturdy build, and her sun and wind-reddened cheeks shone with the healthy glow of the country dweller. Without more ceremony she took me to my room, suggesting I freshen up while she prepared the lunch. Mike was busy on the farm and wouldn't be joining us until the evening.

Over lunch she explained to me how she came to take over the farm. She was the second of three children. When her older brother, Will, had announced that he wanted to emigrate to New Zealand, her father had not objected. Lennie, her younger brother who had been named after his grandfather, had helped on the farm since his youngest days and was keen to take on the responsibility when John decided it was time to hang up his boots.

'Sadly,' she said, 'that day never came. One day – he was just sixteen – Dad asked him to take a tractor up to some woodland on the edge of the farm and drag some felled tree trunks down to one of the barns. Well, evening came and Lennie wasn't back, so my dad went in search of him... He found him dead beneath the tractor. According to the coroner, the rear wheel had slipped off the edge of a track that had been cut into the steep hillside, toppling over and crushing poor Lennie beneath it.'

'Goodness, what a terrible thing.'

'I was eighteen at the time. Young and fancy-free,' Rosie told me. 'But dealing with my parents' grief... with my own grief... made me grow up very quickly. And I was lucky, a couple of years later, to meet Mike, who worked on his father's smallholding. We got married and moved into the dairy at the far end of the farmhouse, which Dad had converted into very comfortable living quarters. And it was agreed that when Dad wanted to pass on management of the farm, we would take it on jointly... And it has worked pretty well. Though these are not easy days for farmers.'

After lunch she took me into the large sitting room. She had dug out a photo album and was now sitting next to me on the sofa. 'They didn't take many photos. People didn't in those days, did they? An expensive business. And wartime, of course. It was only really on big occasions when the camera came out, my dad told me. But there are some here you'll be interested in.'

She opened the album: thick, charcoal-coloured pages; small prints with serrated edges mounted with corner stickers; the captions below, or to the side, written in white ink. 'Look,' said Rosie. 'This is Christmas 1942.' The Christmas feast looked pretty meagre, simple fare in small measures, in accordance with the straitened circumstances of war, but the faces of the eaters, several adults and four boys, looked happy. 'That's Dad,' she said, pointing to one of the boys, who looked wiry and strong.

And before she got a chance to point out anyone else, I spotted the unmistakeable figure of Carlo, grinning diffidently into the lens. 'And there's Carlo... Charlie,' I said. He was sitting next to John, Rosie's father, in a large armchair, bare legs stretching horizontally towards the camera, so that the feet looked disproportionately huge. John, who would have been twelve, looked older than his years; he had an arm around Carlo's shoulder. On the floor in front of them was a tractor made out of blocks of wood. 'Dad made that for Charlie for a Christmas present!'

'Did he talk much about Charlie?'

'Not especially. Mainly only when he was talking about the war. The war years were good for farming. The 1930s had been impossible, and then things picked up. The country had to feed itself, so prices rose once again. The farm got a good price for its milk, most of which was turned into dried milk. There was no refrigeration, so dried milk was essential, especially for the troops. And the farm had pigs. They were easy to feed, and when you slaughtered and salted them you had food for a very long time... But one of the things that upset my grandfather, I know, was that lots of old fields had to be ploughed up for crops, wild meadows and stuff and, once you've lost natural fields, ancient farmland, it's gone forever.'

In reminiscing on her father's and grandfather's talk about the war, Rosie seemed to have forgotten that it was Carlo I had asked about. 'And how did Charlie fit into all this?'

'Ah yes. Charlie! I'm sorry, I was getting carried away with my father's memories... Charlie was very helpful. Very keen to help where he could. Collecting the eggs, shooting rabbits when he was a little older.' Rosie flipped a couple of pages in the album. And there was a picture of Carlo, perhaps aged nine or ten, looking very fit and strong and carrying a shotgun, holding it carefully with the barrel pointing safely toward the ground.

Rosie chuckled. 'Charlie was, by all accounts, a lot more helpful than the Land Girls who were requisitioned. Apparently there were always one or two on the farm. And they were hopeless. Absolutely hopeless! No idea how to milk a cow or anything.'

'And do you know how Charlie came to be with you? What was the story there?'

'He was a sad little waif, according to Dad. Arrived one day with very little warning. My father did remember that very well. The morning Charlie appeared for breakfast the first time. Shy, uncertain, frightened probably, and with very little English. He and a relative or nanny who had brought him from Italy. He was an orphan, I gather, and this relative or nanny had been to England before the war and knew my grandmother. She got in touch with Granny when they arrived in England… The nanny stayed for about a week and then had to report to a camp for immigrants somewhere. The family never heard from her again.'

'Gosh. That's sad.'

'Yes, and I think it took a long time for Charlie to settle in. According to Dad he had some strange habits. For example, he took his shoes to bed with him. I don't mean under the bed. In the bed. Like a kind of security blanket. And for months he used to sit by the gate in the yard, waiting, I suppose, waiting for his nanny to come back.'

'My word, the poor boy.'

'And I think he ran away once, looking for her. Was brought home by the police… Sad. But I'm sure his life here was mostly very happy… Now – let me show you this.'

She rose from the sofa and went to a cupboard beside the large fireplace, returning with an old, battered box, about the size of a shoe box. 'It's Charlie you're interested in and I know you'll find this box fascinating. It's Charlie's childhood treasure chest!' She smiled warmly and confidently as she handed me the box.

In blue crayon Carlo had written his name – Charlie – on the lid, the letters large and awkwardly formed. There was some clumsy decoration, in different colours: stars, asterisks, squiggly lines and a crudely drawn cow; and an aeroplane with a bulbous fuselage and what looked like great skis beneath it.

I opened it, full of interest in what it might contain. Rosie was beaming. 'It's been in that cupboard since Charlie left. He didn't take it with him.' With the lid removed the box released a musty smell. It came either from a shred of very worn fabric or a piece of wood that had been carved into the basic shape of a dagger.

I leant over a side table so that I could take out all the objects one by one. The piece of fabric, measuring about nine inches by five, was more frayed on one end than the other; the less-frayed end looked like it had been scrunched up a thousand times: this was clearly a comfort blanket that had seen very good service. It did not smell very pleasant and neither did the small, tattered teddy bear that I withdrew and quickly laid on the table. Less used, perhaps not used at all, was a rosary, with beads made of jade and a crucifix of either silver or silver plate. Next was a small ball, bigger than a squash ball but smaller than a tennis ball. Most of the surface of the red rubber was perished so I handled it very carefully. The wooden dagger, I saw now, had a 'C' carved on its hilt; the letter was not curved, it had been etched in three strokes so that it looked more like an open box tipped on its side. There was a penknife, which presumably had created the crudely carved 'C'. But the last two items were the most interesting; and the most curious. One was a leaflet, on its cover the legend 'Travel by Air' above an artist's impression of a sea plane, below 'Imperial Airways Empire Flying Boats'. On the reverse was a map of the world, with routes indicated by red markings, bold red lines bearing east from the Americas, sweeping up north from Cape Town, cutting across northern India, the Middle East, the Mediterranean to Marseilles and then north to Southampton. The other item was a painted wooden plaque containing a coat of arms. Described in heraldic terms (I would look these up later) it consisted of the arms, supporters and crest within a royal pavilion surmounted by a royal crown and the standard of the House of Savoy-Aosta: a cross argent in a chief gules; a bendy of six or and gules; supporters of two lions or, langued or; an eagle or crowned of the first. Put more simply, this was a red shield with a white cross held by two lions, with a gold eagle and crown above, and framed in a red ermine-lined robe with gold trimmings.

Lining the bottom of the box, rather more mundanely, was a cotton bag with drawstrings, and embroidered with the same coat of arms.

'This is absolutely fascinating! Thank you so much for showing it to me, Rosie… Do you know much about it?'

'No, I don't. My father never mentioned it. It lay in the cupboard along with lots of other accumulated junk and I didn't discover it until I moved into this part of the house after my father's death.'

'How long did Carlo… Charlie live here?'

'I think he moved out when my father got married. That was in 1956. He left round about then, I'm pretty sure, maybe a little later. From what I can gather, there were tensions. I think Charlie was a difficult teenager! Moody – fairly typical, I guess! Apparently he loved the new music, rock and roll! And when he started working on the farm properly, when he left school, he started buying the kind of clothes you didn't normally see on a farm.' Rosie laughed.

'He was a bit of a Teddy Boy for a while, I gather! Didn't go down well with Grandpa! I know that he found him a handful and was probably relieved when Charlie eventually just upped and awayed.'

'And went where?'

'I'm sorry, Nick, but I really don't know... I think he went to London. He would have been in his early twenties at the time.'

'Were Charlie and your father close?'

'Not that close. Dad spoke quite affectionately about him... But there was a five-year age difference. It was my grandmother who doted on him. And Grandpa in the early days. They had taken him in, this poor little orphan child, this abandoned foreigner. They gave him shelter and security.'

*

Later in the afternoon Rosie gave me a tour of the farm. As we approached the field where the pigs were kept, a couple of geese, in an adjacent space, came bustling towards us, flapping their wings and hissing and honking. The pigs, too, came rushing to us, but were entirely welcoming; they thought we came bearing food. 'What lovely-looking creatures!' I said. 'What breed are they?'

'Gloucester Old Spots. And very delicious, too. I must give you some of our sausages before you go tomorrow. In autumn we collect acorns from the woods for them. Mike insists it improves the taste, and I'm sure he's right.'

In some further fields there were cows grazing with vacant contentment and, as we swept back towards the house, we passed a very large chicken run. The chickens, too, were expecting food and clucked at us indignantly when we ignored them.

I could imagine Carlo growing up here, enjoying the routine of collecting the eggs, of being amongst the sheep and cows and pigs, over the years becoming English in this quintessential landscape.

*

At about six o'clock Mike came in. He was a small, sinewy man, beginning to lose his hair, black speckled with grey. He gave a kindly smile as he looked me in the eye and shook my hand firmly. 'You two been having a good old natter?' he asked.

'Yes. And useful. And wonderful to see that box of young Charlie's treasures.'

'Ah yes. Rosie dug it out last night. It's been in the cupboard for as long as anyone can remember.'

We talked a bit more about Carlo over supper. Both Rosie and Mike were interested in his children and said that they would be most welcome to visit to see where their father had spent his childhood years. I explained that things were a little fraught at the moment, but in time I was sure that would be a good idea.

And we talked about writing, too. Rosie wondered whether I had ever wanted to be a novelist.

'Beyond me, I've always felt. It requires a particular kind of imagination to create and develop and sustain a story over several hundred pages. You see, I'm not really a thinker and I'm not especially imaginative. I'm the medium, not the message, the radio not the broadcaster. I receive and transmit, I don't invent. So I am happy telling the stories of others. They give me the plot and the characters, the incidents... so I don't have to invent anything!'

Mike's expression suggested he was not fully engaging in the conversation. Rosie, though, appeared interested. 'It must be fascinating mixing with all these famous people,' she said. 'I remember when Prince Charles came to visit the village some years ago... It was a wonderful occasion. Everybody turned out to see this famous man. Everyone was happy and cheerful to have someone important here, to be within touching distance of celebrity.'

'Yes, I can see that,' I said. 'Touching distance. That's it, isn't it? Clutching at the hem of fame to feel its transformative power. To touch a little sparkle of magic.'

'Sorry to interrupt, Nick, but, Mike, can you just check to see I've set the recorder for *Strictly*?'

I sensed that this was an attempt to release Mike from the table, a suspicion confirmed by the obvious relief with which he sprang up.

'Don't let me keep you from your programme.'

'No, it's fine. We're recording it. I think. So... are you transformed by your closeness to celebrity?'

'No! I don't think so. And most celebrities are as ordinary as the rest of us, and that's what people tend to forget. I remember chatting once to a journalist from one of the quality dailies. He'd been an MP before turning to journalism. He quickly made his name as a columnist. This got him appearances on television, mainly current affairs programmes—'

'Would I know of him?'

I told her his name. She shook her head.

'Well, there you are, not a household name, by any means. But he told me once that because your name was "out there", as he put it, people made assumptions about you. They think you are special, not realising that you are not in the least bit special, that you have exactly the same inadequacies and insecurities that ordinary people have... People have such odd notions of celebrity. Are obsessed with it. Do you know, I was invited back to my old school a couple of years ago to give a talk to the sixth form about freelance writing as a career. And when it came to questions at the end, I thought they'd be asking about entry paths into the business, or suitable work experience, that kind of thing, but actually the only thing the kids were interested in was the celebrities I had met or written about!'

'Fascinating! ...Well, look, let's have some coffee... Are you a *Strictly* fan?'

'Not really. But happy to watch it, if that's what you'd like.'

'Good. Well, let's catch up with the end of it then.' She was following a comedian who had grown up locally and whose shtick made much of his Devonian roots. 'He is wonderful, you know. So funny. And some dancer! Everyone around here is hoping he will win... or at least get to the final.'

When we got to the sitting room we found a dozing Mike and, trying not to disturb him, sat to watch the celebrities strut their stuff.

Later in the evening – Mike had gone to bed by this stage – I told Rosie about Carlo's confabulated past. She was riveted by my story and seemed understand completely the urge to reinvent himself, the waif who had arrived in England with nothing but his pitiful treasure chest. 'And if you were going to reinvent yourself,' she said, 'why wouldn't you become a prince? The Frog Prince! And why wouldn't you want part of your story to be about how you were at the heart of a really interesting time in history?'

17

That night at Highfold Farm, before I fell asleep, I turned over in my mind the events of the day, thinking how it would have thrilled Theresa to have visited the farmhouse. How she would have loved to walk over the land that her father had walked as a young boy; and what extraordinary pleasure it would have given her to see and to touch the collection of objects that had belonged to Carlo, his 'treasure chest', as Rosie had called it. I could see the Theresa I had known at the start of our association bubbling away with excitement, bombarding Rosie with all kinds of questions.

As Angelo and Helen Goretti had been, Rosie too was keen to meet Carlo's children, and was happy for them to come and stay at the farm as I had done. But that was not to be. Not for the time being, at any rate, and perhaps never. After my visit to the Gorettis I had rung Luca to say that I was making some progress in finding out about Carlo's earlier life.

I was taken aback by his response. 'Nick, this is of no interest to me, and I do not want you unsettling Theresa any further.' Luca had always seemed the epitome of calmness and of gentle good manners. But there was hostility in his voice now, anger even. 'She is not in a good way and I repeat, I do not want you upsetting her further.'

'Luca, I have never meant to upset her. Never, at any stage... I thought you both wanted me to find out as much as I could about your father.'

'Well, that may have been what she originally wanted, but it is not any more. Nor I. I would like to terminate whatever arrangement you think you had with Theresa. If you have any expenses to be paid, please invoice me.'

'Okay, Luca. I'll do that.'

'And please, Nick, do not attempt to see Theresa again. She says you have been pestering her.'

I realised there was no point protesting my innocence. Theresa, immured in her wall of unreason, had obviously said things to her brother – things that simply weren't true – and he was taking them at face value. I could have protested, but I didn't want to. I didn't want to intrude on a relationship that was important to both the siblings as they grappled with their grief for their dead father.

'No, I won't get in touch. Don't worry.'

'...And that photographer who sometimes lurks outside her flat... If he's got anything to do with you, call him off. Otherwise I shall have to take action on Theresa's behalf.'

It didn't immediately occur to me that Luca might have been referring to George Nelson. 'Absolutely nothing to do with me, Luca, I can assure you.'

*

Three days later I had a phone call from George himself. He was in Charing Cross Hospital, sounding as sorry for

197

himself as I had ever heard him. Actually he had never sounded sorry for himself before and even now, as he lay in a hospital bed with a broken collarbone, a fractured leg and two broken ribs, he did not sound completely downhearted. He wanted me to visit him.

When I arrived, he shouted an expansive 'Nickolai!' And then, as he spotted the gift I had brought him, his welcoming beam dimmed to a look of disbelief. 'Grapes? Grapes, me old son? For me? Strike a light! Nurse, help me, help me, I'm being graped!' he cried in mock alarm.

'Have you not had any other visitors, George?'

'Only inmates. Passing by… Bum-sniffing.'

'Bum-sniffing?'

'You know. Dogs. Sniff each other's bums. "How's yer diddling?" Sniff sniff. "Where's yer been?" Sniff sniff. "Wotcha bin eating?" Sniff sniff. "Fancy a bit of rumpy pumpy?" Sniff sniff. That kinda thing.'

'George, what are you talking about?'

'Dogs, mate. But it's the same with people. Bum-sniffing. "Weather's not so good, today." "Oh, I know, I know. Terrible." "See that Boris has been up to his old tricks again." "I know, I know, but what can you do?" "Soon be outta here, old feller." "I hope so, I hope so." Bum-sniffing. Small talk. Chit-chat. I hate it!'

'Well, let's talk business, then, George. What on earth has happened to you?' I asked.

He was propped up on a bank of pillows, one arm in a sling, strapping around his chest; a heavily plastered leg was elevated on a pillow. 'Came off the back of a motorbike. Nudged by a car. As it 'appens, not going too fast. Otherwise I would of banged me bonce as well.'

'Where did this happen, George?'

He came over all sheepish. And I realised in an instant that he was the photographer Luca had been talking about. 'Erm… Well… Er, 'Ammersmith Grove, as it 'appens.'

'And why were you there?'

Even more sheepish. 'Just business… you know… earning me crust—'

'George, who were you after? Which celeb?'

'Erm—'

'George, you tell me, or I'll walk out of here and never see you again.'

'Okay. Okay. Thing is, Nick, ever since the funeral, I've had this thing about the d'Abruisee girl. I don't know why. She's so beautiful… I guess I just got a crush on 'er… And she's very photogenic.'

'Christ, man, you've been stalking the poor woman.'

George let out a pained moan. 'Oh God, don't do this to me now, Nick. I'm in enough pain as it is.'

'And trouble.' I was about to continue when another visitor appeared by George's bed, directed by one of the nurses.

'Georgie! What on earth has happened to you?'

George looked at me and then at his visitor, a smartly dressed, well-spoken woman probably in her late sixties. He looked startled. Then panicked. Then embarrassed.

With a shifty and awkward look, he said, 'Got clattered by a motor-scooter… mmu… erm… Hilary.'

'Poor you! Poor, poor you!' There was a crackling of paper as she dug into a Waitrose carrier bag and pulled out a packet. 'I've brought you some grapes, George. Vitamin C. Full of healing properties.'

The look of embarrassment on George's face deepened as he meekly accepted the gift. He smiled weakly. 'Oh, erm, thank you. Thank you… Just the ticket!' The cockney vowels had been strangely flattened, straight-jacketed into what was almost a Standard English accent.

The woman continued in her cut-glass accent. 'I always used to buy you grapes when you got ill as a child, George, do you remember?'

George's eyes closed in resignation.

I must have done a double-take. 'Excuse me, I don't think we've been introduced.'

'No. How rude of you, George! Where were you dragged up?'

I held out my right hand in greeting. 'Nick Barry.'

'Hilary. Hilary Nelson.' As George groaned half in pain, half in wretched embarrassment, she added, 'George's mother.'

Later in the day George would ring me to explain. 'Explain' was the word he used. 'That little ol' lady wot you met at the 'ospital? Right ol' joker, she is. Me muvver! Me muvver? Would you Adam and Eve it, Nickolai? She is a little ol' lady from the local church doing good works – visiting the 'alt and the lame in 'ospital, God bless her! Pretending she was me muvver! Yer gotta laugh, ain't yer?'

*

I was finishing off my revised piece for George, the article to accompany the photo project that would supposedly launch him on a more reputable career path. That had been the purpose of the summons to Charing Cross Hospital.

Trussed up like a chicken about to be basted, he knew that he would be unable to do any work until his bones had mended, so was keen to get his new incarnation up and running in the meantime.

'I'm definitely giving up this pap malarkey, Nick me old son. Trust me. But you gotta get my story out there. Quickly.'

A neighbour held one of his spare front-door keys and George had arranged for him to go to his computer, transfer a copy of his Thames photoshoot folder onto a data stick and get it over to me. My instructions then were to revise my original draft of the story, which I had written as some kind of therapy on the day that Carlo had died, select a maximum of ten of the photos, caption them, write a summary of the project and bring my finished piece to him in hospital for approval. Unless he was already out. He couldn't bear being confined and was talking about discharging himself.

I quickly redid and expanded my original piece. I left it more as less as it was, changing the words George had said he would never use, trying to capture his distinctive voice more exactly. The expansion was brief, but I felt it was important; George had told me in a recent discussion that the piece had to be true to himself. So I added what I had withheld in the first piece. That he had been a paparazzo for some of his career.

The paragraph where he – I – had said that he had spent some years taking photographs of the great and good but had got bored by the sameyness of it all, now contained an admission of his murkier exploits.

Over the years I took photographs of the great and the good. And it paid the bills, make no mistake. But then, I thought – after some years, mind – that photographing celebrities was good for bringing in the dosh but was becoming a bit samey. I said to myself, 'George, me old mucker, you're getting stuck in a rut, son!'

That rut, if I'm honest – and my dear old mum always told me to be honest, so I've always tried to be – did include some pics that were, well, taken without the subject's permission. Sometimes, perhaps, without their knowledge. Yes, some people regarded me as a pap, the lowest of the low. And that's what I was. So when I say I was getting stuck in a rut, it was sometimes more than a rut, it was a ditch! Or a prickly bush! And I wanted out.

I spent a long time selecting the right photographs. There were so many to choose from and so many good ones with genuine artistic merit. It was easy to illustrate George's skill as a photographer. Finally I chose those pictures that most fully contributed to the narrative of the river sequence. I then wrote an introductory paragraph.

Writing captions was even more difficult. This was a job normally left to a sub-editor, but whoever would finalise the captions needed the basic information. The problem lay not so much in coming up with pithy summaries of each selected photo, but with making sense of George's handwritten notes, neat though they were.

*

He was discharged the following day. I imagine that the nurses were relieved to be rid of him. He did not strike me as the ideal patient. An impatient inpatient rather than a patient. So I drove over to see him in Chiswick. The door was answered by a carer who he'd hired from some probably very expensive local agency. She was a young, attractive Romanian woman called Martina. She led me to the front room where George was throned on a wing chair, propped up with pillows, his injured leg resting on a footstool.

'Nick, me old mucker! You got the goods, mate?'

He made it sound like some exchange of illicit dealings in the back room of a pub, rather than the transfer of a carefully crafted piece of journalism which was going to change his life for the better.

'I have.' I had printed out the piece in the way I envisaged it appearing in a magazine.

After asking Martina to bring us drinks, he read through it, peering at the photographs critically, reading the copy slowly. 'This is blooming good, mate!' he said. 'Even the bit about me being a pap! More of a ditch than a rut! Love it!' He grinned.

'Not much rutting for you in your current condition, though, is there, George!' I said mischievously.

What began as a howl of laughter quickly turned into an agonised bellow. 'Aaaaarrrgh! ...Christ, Nick, don't make me laugh, it hurts like buggery!' He began to laugh again, but checked himself, grimacing. 'As for rutting, Nichol-arse, that's off the menu for the time being... But Martina, here' – he gave a grotesquely exaggerated wink and tapped the side of his nose – 'she might have to take me in 'and if I'm a naughty boy!'

It didn't bear thinking about. So I asked him about the accident. 'What on earth happened, George? Are you getting careless in your old age?'

'I think I was bumped off, mate.' He started a laugh but quickly reined it in. 'Not literally bumped off! Otherwise I wouldn't be here! I'd be a ghost… Like you, Nick! Ghost! Geddit?' This time he couldn't stop himself, emitting an unsettling cacophony of chortle and agonised groan.

'It wasn't an accident, you mean?'

'Nah. I don't think so. I think someone was trying to… discourage me.'

'Why do you think that?'

'I saw the driver looking at me. Angrily. 'E knew what 'e was doing. I don't think 'e wanted to kill me, just nudge me off the bike to scare me away. Me mate, who was driving the bike, was fucking furious!'

'Do you know who it was?'

'Nah.'

'Did you catch the number plate?'

'Yeah.'

'So you know who it is. You've asked your tame plod?'

'Nah. Not interested. It comes with the territory, mate… You go nosing around, you get in a few scrapes. All's fair, etcetera.'

The unsettling words of Luca were now rattling around my head. He had said something like, if the photographer that was pestering Theresa was anything to do with me – a preposterous thought – I should call him off. Otherwise he would have to take action. Luca, of course, was a lawyer, so I had assumed that by 'action' he had meant legal action. I was sure that he would never descend to any other kind of action.

'George, do lots of celebrities live around Hammersmith Grove?'

'Sure, mate. Very fashionable area these days.'

'So you could have been bumped off—'

'Don't you start, mate. My ribs won't take it!'

'What I was going to say was, you could have been nudged off by the minder of a number of people.'

'Sure. Sure.'

'You weren't outside Theresa's flat.'

'Nah. Not then.'

'And you promise me that you'll never try to photograph her again?'

He cocked his head and gave me a sceptical sidelong glance.

I picked up the article and held it as though I was about to tear it up. 'You'll never see this or me again, George, if you don't promise.'

'Okay, mate. I promise.' He marked a hurried cross on his chest with his forefinger. 'And 'ope to die, mate.'

*

I had taken one worry away from Theresa, the pestering George Nelson. And Luca had taken another, the supposedly pestering Nick Barry, warning me to stay away from her.

As I drove back to Kingston, I felt a real sense of loss. It was strange. I hadn't known Theresa for long, but I realised now that it was a relationship that had become very important to me. It didn't feel completely like love. Although we'd had sex together, that had been almost incidental. Transactional, even. But she had touched me in some way. The enormous, flooding energy of her enthusiasm, her zest, had charged me in some way. Perhaps I had, after all, unwittingly fallen in love with her. And to know of her terrible pain now, to have seen that remarkable vigour bled out of her, was unbearable. What crystallised for me as I drove home was the realisation that I, too, felt a pain, the pain of exile. Luca had exiled me.

18

I had lunch the next day with Chalky White. Chalky had been a big name in the music business before moving into the film world. After university he had drifted around Europe and the Near East in a beat-up old Land Rover, doing odd jobs to get by, exploring places he'd never dreamt of, observing and enjoying cultures different from his own. Having fulfilled his wanderlust for the time being, he ended up, for no particular reason, in Dublin. Here, with a university friend, in one of the run-down lanes by the docks, he had created and developed a recording studio. With hard work and good fortune, he very quickly created a very successful business. A local rock group, in its own infancy, had found the fledgling studios convenient and had continued to record there when they had become, in a remarkably short period of time, one of the biggest acts in the business, global superstars filling arenas around the world. In time, the music studio would become a place of pilgrimage for fans, who could be found on most days milling around outside, hoping for the glimpse of a rock-star hero, normally having to settle for no more than a close inspection of the colourfully graffitied outer walls of the building.

When Chalky White sold his share in the studio he made an absolute killing. Moving back to England he had decided to go into film production. His first movie was a gentle, whimsical story about an English crooner who had been big in the fifties before being swept away in the early 1960s by the tsunami of Liverpudlian pop groups. The story-line saw him being hunted down by an erstwhile fan, dragged out of contented retirement, and brought into a limelight of sorts with a tour of venues around the country. The story was strong, the music fabulous and the theme – an essay on the relationship between fame and contented anonymity – interestingly explored. The film had been released at just the right time. There was a nostalgic audience seeking feel-good schmaltz. It did well, and Chalky's new career quickly became as successful as his old one. Chalky White was definitely a name in the cultural firmament of the 1990s and the noughties.

He had now written an autobiography. His own life had been interesting, with his post-university travels and his Midas touch in the music and film businesses. And he wrote with insight about the people he had worked with: the technical people at various levels, the money men, the film people and the rock stars, who ranged from the dully ordinary to the extraordinarily bizarre.

As it happened, he had the same literary agent as me and, when he had presented his manuscript to her, Vikki had told him that it was most definitely sellable but needed a significant rewrite. Chalky was much too busy for that, he said. Which was when Vikki proposed that I was just the person to do the rewrite for him. Hence the lunch, the three of us meeting in an expensively pleasant eatery in the West End.

I mention all this, not because Chalky White is an integral part of my story about Carlo and Luca and Theresa, because he isn't. I write about him because he could have been and perhaps would have been, if Carlo had been who he said he was. If I had met Chalky a few months earlier, when I was exploring the version of her father that Theresa had given me, I would have told him that I had some great material for a wonderful movie. I would have mapped out my film treatment for him: a young boy of royal descent, orphaned in the war years and fleeing to England; growing up on a West Country farm; his years of intellectual growth studying in New York; the romantic decision to take to the sea; discovering the raw vitality of a rejuvenated Hamburg; the Epstein story; the Albert Hall event; bringing the radical *International Times* to the streets of London; his abandonment of the febrile delights of London for the challenge of teaching young minds in the bracing sea air of the south coast.

I would have explained to him how I would have written the screenplay, with a framing device of the lecturing years: scenes of the mature Carlo's university incarnation intercut with his life story, the boy Carlo, the escape across Europe, the young man Carlo; and the further intercutting, where appropriate, of contemporary film footage – of the grey post-war years, the Beatles' explosion, Ginsberg at the Albert Hall, The Doors at the Roundhouse.

This, after all, was how Theresa had envisaged the movie. And as I sat with Vikki and Chalky, discussing the autobiography, it was Theresa's presence I felt most strongly. Or her absence. And the absence – the non-existence, to be more precise – of the story I so would have liked to tell Chalky.

So, sadly, because there was nothing to tell, I told him nothing. Nevertheless, the lunch went well and we came to a workable agreement over Chalky's book. It would keep me busy and ensure a few more months of comfortable existence. And would help me to forget about Theresa.

*

The phone. It was Rosie Barlow. She sounded in a state of high excitement, her voice liquid, flooding down the line like a stream in spate.

'Nick! You'll never guess what! We've made an extraordinary find. Two extraordinary finds! Mike and me. Taking that treasure chest of Charlie's out from the cluttered cupboard in the sitting room, when you were down, prompted Mike and me to start a clear-out of the attic. My goodness, there was so much junk up there! Years and years of it. Unlooked at. Untouched. Old farm ledgers, trunks of ancient clothes, dusty pictures with cracked glass, old toys. Gosh, so much stuff. All kinds of stuff!'

I was wondering where all this was going. The early excitement of Rosie's voice had given way to an undercurrent of amusement as she detailed her finds in the attic. Trying not to sound impatient, I prompted her. 'And the special things you found?'

'You'll never guess what…' Of course I wouldn't, so I waited for the big reveal. 'We found a diary, a journal kind

210

of thing. It's Rosa's! The nanny. Charlie's nanny who brought him over from Italy!'

And now Rosie had got my interest. It was my turn to feel a flooding excitement, and I was almost shaking. 'Wow!' I said. 'That is incredible! …What kind of things does it say?'

There was a shriek of laughter. 'I haven't a clue, Nick. It's all in Italian! …But we thought that you might be able to translate it… or get it translated—'

'Of course,' I said.

'And the other find is ever more wonderful, Nick. It's a letter from Charlie to my grandparents. A lovely, lovely letter thanking them for bringing him up, apologising for not being in touch for so long. Telling them what he'd been up to.'

'Gosh! That's really interesting. When was it written?'

'Erm, 1966, I think. March, 1966. It was in a small box which had "Keep" written in big letters on the outside. It had various letters in it, with names that meant nothing to me, but as soon as I saw this one from Charlie I said to Mike, "Mike, we've got to tell Nick about this." Which is what I'm doing!' She laughed again.

'That is fantastic, Rosie… Can I come down to see them?'

'Of course. But I'm happy to send them, if you want.'

And that was what we arranged. Leaving me to wait excitedly over the next few days for the postman's knock at the door.

*

I had arranged for Gina, an Italian writer friend of mine, to translate Rosa's journal. I had warned her that I had no idea what to expect of it: the quality of the handwriting; the nature of the language, be it diary shorthand, idiosyncratic note-form, or full commentary; whether there would be issues of dialect – all these things.

I glanced at it quickly when it arrived. It was a ledger, six inches by eight and half inches in size, with about eighty pages of unruled paper. The writing was legible, though of varying quality, some entries sloping at strange angles, suggesting that the writer had sometimes been in awkward positions when composing. All but the last few pages had been used. There was the odd doodle, some lists, an occasional schedule, but mainly the content was diary entries covering a period of nine days, the 8th to the 16th April 1940. I drove this over to Gina on the day it arrived, asking her to get cracking on the translation as quickly as she could.

The letter, of course, presented no such problems. I read it several times, and with each reading was more moved by the man the letter was revealing. It was dated 21st May 1966 and its address was the flat in Herne Hill where Carlo had lived when working at Brixton Library.

> Dear Dora and Len (Mum and Dad of course),
>
> First up, I want to say how sorry I am not to have kept in touch with you all these years. I don't know whether you have worried about me or not, I hope not. All the years you looked after me we never talked about my real mum and dad. I suppose I didn't want to and you didn't want to upset me by talking about them. I don't have any real memories

of them apart from the last day. Thats not what I wanted to remember. But then I suppose I wanted to get away and be on my own and see if other memories came back to me but they didn't. Thats really why I went.

You were very good to me, to take me in and John was like a brother but when he got married I decided it was time to move on. I came to London, don't know what for, to find myself maybe or try. I got a room in Streatham and became a milkman. You'l laugh at that, me out early in the morning delivering bottles of milk rather than seeing to the cows. and then I became a postman in the same area. I enjoyed that, knocking on doors getting to know people and I didn't mind getting up early I was used to it from the milk round and I liked getting home early.

I was never very good at school was I. You both used to tell me I should work hard to have more opportunities, and I shouldve. I'm trying to make up now. I get home from the post office and read, I get books from the library in Brixton. Even poetry!! The beat poets from America and the Liverpool poets, they write real stuff, I understand it and it says something, not like the stuff they gave us at school. And I go to readings, went to a big Happening at the Albert Hall last year, with big names, it was fabulous.

I'm over thirty now, so it might be a bit late, but I want to study, get some diplomas or something so I can better myself. I saved money over the years, don't spend it on much other than clothes, you should see me! and food, and I'm very happy in this flat in Herne Hill.

I hope the farm is going well. I suppose you will be grandparents by now, what lucky children to have people like you. You were very good to me, looking after me like you did. I do want to remember my own parents too and what happened to them but I think I've never realy understood it all, maybe in time.

Give my love to John and his family.

Your everloving
Carlo

ps I changed my name back to Carlo when I came to London, I hope you don't mind.

*

Gina's translation of Rosa's journal arrived a few days later. I skim-read it, read it again and then once more, by which time I knew what I needed to do with it.

The writing was spare, much of it in note form. But it contained the bare bones of a most extraordinary narrative. It started with a brief account of Rosa's past, which included astonishing details of her employment just prior to becoming Carlo Goretti's nanny, details which would have very important consequences on her ability to escape Trieste when the time came. It seems that the journal had been written as much for Carlo as for Rosa herself. She writes about his parents and about her love for the sensitive young boy. There follows a terse, unadorned account of the fate of Bosco, his father, and of the presumed fate of his mother, Maria, and brother, Alfonso. There is no melodrama here, not even any attempt to tug the heartstrings: the tone is factual, objective; and all the more shocking in its understatement.

Most of the journal deals with the hazardous escape from Trieste and the adventures, sometime perilous, of the journey to England. There are different stages to this, none of which are without risk, but all navigated successfully – eventually – by Rosa and her ward.

What emerges painfully from the account is the contained sadness of the traumatised Carlo. And what comes across equally is the remarkable nature of Rosa. Clear foresightedness has provided her with the means to attempt the journey. But to complete it she needed adaptability, quick-wittedness, the ability to manipulate and, above all, resilience. She seemed to have all these qualities in abundance.

As I finished the journal for the third time, I felt a deep excitement, and a sense of mission, too, as I contemplated my next move: to turn this powerful piece of note-taking into a fully imagined narrative.

But first I needed to do a little research. I needed to understand the context of what was happening in the Mediterranean at the time. It turned out that Rosa and Carlo's April escape had been made none too soon. On the 10th May Germany invaded Belgium, Holland and France, France capitulating in barely six weeks. A month after the German invasion, Italy entered the arena, creating in the Mediterranean a new theatre of war for the conflicted protagonists of Europe. By the end of June there were no civilian flights from or across Europe.

When I felt I was ready, I went back to the journal and plotted out the story of Rosa and Carlo, sticking rigidly to the substance of the journal entries while fleshing them out into a fuller narrative. At this stage I was unsure whether I would add a crucial detail that sadly Carlo would never learn and of which presumably Rosa, too, remained ignorant: I had the broader perspective that Angelo Goretti had given me when telling me of that fateful day in April 1940.

PART III

LIFE-LINES

19

ROSA AND CARLO

8th April 1940

Rosa was walking quickly towards the Porto
Vecchio. Quickly, but not too quickly. She
did not want to draw attention to herself.
For the same reason, she was not looking
back. In one hand, clinging on as tightly as
he could, was a little boy. Seen from behind,
nothing would appear untoward in this pair.
A young mother walking to the fishermen's
dock to buy some fish, perhaps. But seen
from the front, the boy surely would have
attracted some attention. His face was pale,
and stretched into a frozen expression of
agony. Or shock, was it? Probably both.
It was a look that would have disturbed
anyone catching sight of the little child; a
look that surely would have invited enquiry,
or solicitation perhaps.

In Rosa's other hand she was clutching

a Gladstone bag, its improvised straps looped over her shoulder. It looked old and somewhat battered, the copper brown sides scuffed, the puckered, in-tucked ends of the bag still retaining their unworn umber colour. She had collected this sturdy carrier from her bank immediately after she and her young charge had fled from the Via Mazzini. Snatching Carlo's hand with a rough urgency, she had dragged him quickly away from the scene of horror she had stumbled upon outside Bosco Goretti's shoe shop.

She was sure that two of the men had seen them. But she dared not look behind her. In any case, she was nearly at the dock. If only she could get to Matteo, she felt sure she would be safe. She quickened her pace a little, coaxing Carlo, who had said nothing since being dragged away from his father's shop, to keep up with her. Finally she was there, at Matteo's fish stall. She asked if he could leave the stall a moment and walk with her so that she could be unheard by anyone else. Her agitation was threatening to erupt into hysteria, but with a forced calmness she told him what had just happened, described the horror that she and Carlo has just witnessed.

Matteo's assistant, unable to hear the conversation, would have seen the instant shock in his employer's face; would have seen a woman whose name he could not remember lean forward and hold out her upturned palms in a gesture of supplication; would have seen Matteo pull a scrap of paper from his pocket and write a few sentences on it.

Once more she took the hand of the silent child, more gently this time, thanked Matteo, and started walking back to towards potential danger. She had been told to go to the Canale Grande, to the Ponte Rosso, not far from Bosco's shop. She chose back streets and side streets. Twice she turned into a shop entrance or the doorway of a house to wait to see whether she was being followed.

As she led Carlo up the Via Vincenzo Bellini, she hoped the boat she was seeking would not be too far up the canal. The open space of the Piazza del Ponte Rosso would make them more visible. More vulnerable. Unfortunately, the small red-hulled craft, the *Mariana*, was not far from the bridge, in full view of the piazza. She decided that she would just have to hope for the best, and began to walk towards it, trying to look as confident as possible.

When she got there, she peered down and shouted, 'Enzo... Enzo.' No reply. Perhaps he was not on the boat after all. She bent down to rap on the roof of the cabin and called again; she could hear a stirring. There was a rattle of the cabin door, and a bleary-eyed, unshaven man appeared, looking quizzically at his unexpected visitors.

'Enzo,' Rosa said. 'I've got a message for you. Can we come on board?'

'S'pose so,' he said in a sleepy drawl.

*

As the *Mariana* pulled out of the harbour, Rosa wondered if she would ever again see the hills that curved protectively around Trieste, where only the previous summer Bosco and Maria had taken her and the family for a memorable picnic. She had always known that one day she might have to flee the city and that she might have very little time to make her escape. That was why she had deposited the Gladstone bag at the bank, ready for a speedy collection and hurried flight. Within one compartment there was a change of clothes and some dried meat and chocolate bars; in a small interior pocket was a bone-handled sheaf knife, unsheathed. The other compartment contained a pencil, a blank notebook with unlined pages, documents and, beneath a cardigan, money – a great deal of money. Tucked away at the bottom were three mysterious objects, talismanic objects that she thought might save her life.

The quickest way out of the city would have been by train, but Rosa had worried that the station might be being watched. In the brief moment that she and Carlo had approached Bosco's shop, she had heard one of the thugs sending two of his henchmen to the Goretti house. 'Take care of them,' he had shouted in an ugly, brutal voice. She was assuming the worst. And was wondering how on earth she would be able to explain to Carlo that he had lost his entire family in a single day.

So here she was, Carlo at her side, sailing towards Venice, as arranged with Enzo. The boat was small but had a powerful inboard engine which was cutting effortlessly through a calm sea. Trieste quickly diminished into a tiny speck on the horizon before disappearing altogether. The sky above was cloudless, a brilliant blue, and the motion of the boat on the waves was pleasant and calming. Carlo, still wordless, had relaxed a little. The taut face loosened as he began to settle into the adventure of a trip out to sea.

Rosa had never been to Venice, but when it came into view, with its towers, campaniles and domes, it seemed very familiar. Enzo did not want to go deep into the lagoon and dropped his travellers at the jetty on the small island of San Pietro di Castello. The walk to the Santa Lucia station was long and slow and arduous for the tired and traumatised boy. They stopped a few times, either for Rosa to ask for directions or for Carlo to rest a little. When he was offered food by Rosa he nodded his head but maintained the silence that had remained unbroken from the moment he and his nanny had begun their flight from Trieste.

By the time they arrived at the station, its unadorned rectangular flatness a surprise to Rosa amidst the Gothic flamboyance of the city, there were no trains to Livorno, nor to Florence where they would need to change.

'I'm sorry, Carlo, we're going to have to spend the night here. I'm so sorry, my darling boy.'

He started to cry, the first sounds he'd made since the morning. Rosa drew him to her, stroking his head, his face, his shoulders and led him towards a bench. There she laid him down with his head on her lap. Then she took some of her clothes from the Gladstone bag and covered him. Soon he was in a fitful sleep, crying out a couple of times.

Rosa had lengthened the two shoulder straps of the bag so that she could loop them around her waist and then put her hand around Carlo's arm to reassure him of her presence throughout the night. She had intended to maintain a steady watchfulness, but couldn't help dozing off a couple of times, awoken by some sound or by a sudden movement of the boy.

9th April 1940

The next evening, after an uneventful journey, Rosa found a lodging house in Livorno, close to the docks. Carlo had gazed with interest as the train had pulled out the station in Venice, but had soon withdrawn into himself once more, eventually sleeping, leaving Rosa to reflect on the previous twenty-four hours.

From the moment she and Carlo had wandered down to Bosco's shop, stumbling on the unexpected scene, everything had happened so quickly: the hurried turn-about, the rush to the bank, the quick walk to the fishermen's docks, the boat journey to Venice. So far, the escape had gone as she had hoped. But England was still a very a long way off. Once on the *Mariana*, and safely out to sea, Rosa had checked her Gladstone bag to see that it contained everything she needed: the money she had stolen, the talismans she had taken from the same household, the piece of paper on which she had outlined possible routes to England. And an address in England, her journey's end, she hoped:

Abbott
Highfold Farm
Stowford
Nr Okehampton
Devon

It was while she was on the train that she started her journal. The first pages were about herself. Rosa Drago: born in Ancona, where she grew up in a large family. Rosa

Drago, who in her late teens had gone to England to train as a nanny.

10th April 1940

She had risen early and left Carlo in the care of the landlady of the lodging house while she went to the docks to try to find a boat that would take her on the next stage of the journey. Leaving her Gladstone bag and money belt behind, she had taken only the portion of money she was prepared to spend. It was a healthy sum, but it took time and a great deal of searching before she was able to secure a fisherman to take her and Carlo to Corsica.

She collected the boy and headed back towards the boat. As they approached the dock and passed the Quattro Mori, Carlo tugged her arm, bringing her to a standstill. He was pointing, not at the stone sculpture poised assertively on the top of the statue, but at the four bronze figures of the Moorish slaves chained uncomfortably with their arms behinds their backs to each corner of the plinth.

'What are they doing?' he asked with an expression of disturbed fascination on his face. 'It's not nice, is it?'

'No, I suppose not, my darling boy,' she said. 'But it's from a long time ago. Nothing to worry about.'

'I don't like it.' He tugged her again, this time drawing her away.

The fisherman who was to take them to Bastia was called Bruno, a grizzled, taciturn man who seemed to prefer gesture to words. He nodded his passengers into the cabin and nosed his craft past the formidable pink solidity of the Fortezza Vecchio towards the harbour mouth. It was a bigger boat than the *Mariana* and was decked with the bits and pieces that were a fisherman's stock in trade: pots, tubs, nets, lines, a winch, a ladder. The deck was protected by a bent canopy of warped plywood, with dirty awnings flapping down the sides. Carlo was fascinated. When Rosa asked Bruno if the boy could sit on deck amongst the assemblage of fishing gear, he gave a shrug and a nod.

There was cloud in the sky today and a brisk breeze. The sea was less calm than on the journey they had taken two days earlier; Carlo looked distinctly queasy but resisted being sick.

As they approached the fishermen's dock in Bastia, Rosa asked Bruno if they would be able find a boat to take them to Marseilles.

He shrugged. 'Maybe.' Then opened his hands out in front of him. 'Or maybe Toulon... Easier.'

'From Bastia?'

Again the gesture of the hands. 'Who knows?' There was a silence. 'Maybe Saint-Florent is better.'

He went into the cabin, rootled around

for a moment, found a notepad and pencil, and wrote something down. When he came out again he stubbed the piece of paper with a dirty finger and handed it to Rosa.

'These people, perhaps,' he said. 'Ask for them. In Saint-Florent.'

*

Rosa and Carlo were being driven out of Bastia in a dusty limousine, a Citroen Traction Avant 7. A ray of light had shone through Carlo's pained face when he had seen the car. He immediately reached out with his little arm so that he could touch one of the two huge headlamps perched on the large mudguards that swept gracefully from the front of the long bonnet. And then he was ushered into the backseat of the car.

After leaving Bruno's boat, Rosa had gone into a dockside café to ask where she might find someone to drive her and her little boy to Saint-Florent, about fourteen miles away. It wasn't long before she had her volunteer. 'I'm going that way,' a man calling himself Pietro had said. 'Wait here and I'll get the car.'

While he was away, Rosa bent down to Carlo and whispered in his ear. 'Remember, little one, the words I will say to warn you of danger: "Red fire engine".' He nodded. 'When I say that, you must act quickly and do exactly as I say.' He nodded again.

Rosa sat in the front of the car, with her bag beneath her knees; Carlo, short legs outstretched before him, was on the back seat, gazing out of the window as the car climbed steeply up the Serra di Pigno's winding road. The landscape was rocky and scrubby, the distant sea below flashing into view every now and again.

And then began the long, gradual descent down to Saint-Florent. Like Bruno, Pietro seemed a man of few words. Rosa was happy not to talk, content to enjoy the peace of the drive, but after a while she became aware of a strange, muted sense of agitation in the man, and she noticed that his eyes were darting sideways every now and again to glance at her knees and at the bag beneath them.

Shortly after they had driven through a straggling village, Pietro, making a strange, half-suppressed coughing sound, turned off the Saint-Florent road onto a track that led steeply up a wooded hillside.

'What are you doing? ...Stop!' Rosa cried.

He just stared ahead, driving on.

Rosa glanced over her shoulder. 'Red fire engine!' Bringing Carlo, who had been leaning lazily against the door, to an upright position, alert, confused and frightened. And awaiting any instructions.

Pietro glanced at Rosa with an irritated frown on his face. 'What? What do you mean "red fire engine"?'

Deftly, before he could react, Rosa opened her bag and withdrew the sheaf knife. With a quick, single movement she leant towards him, arched her arm over his shoulder and pricked the point of the knife into his neck.

He tried to move his body away, took a hand from the wheel and grabbed her arm. She pushed the knife into the skin just below his Adam's apple, immediately drawing blood. As he tugged her arm, trying to pull it away, she jerked him towards her, causing the knife to penetrate more deeply.

In the back, Carlo was groaning in panic.

'Turn this fucking car around and take me to the main road.'

The car had swerved as Pietro had tugged at Rosa's arm and she had pulled at him. He instinctively grabbed the steering wheel with both hands and steadied the vehicle. She tightened her grip around his neck and adjusted the knife to a position on the jugular. She had his blood on her sleeve now. But she was prepared to spill more.

'Turn this fucking car around and take me to the main road or I'll fucking kill you.' She was screaming now.

'Okay, okay... Okay.'

11th April 1940

It was a clear night, the nearly full moon dancing an arrhythmical pattern on the waves of the Mediterranean. Carlo was asleep on a bench in the cabin of the *Hibernian Heron,* Rosa standing beside Brian Boucher as he guided his fishing boat towards Toulon.

After an anxious night in a small lodging house in Saint-Florent, she had gone to the docks early the next morning in search of either Brian or Franco. These were the names on Bruno's scrap of paper. It was Brian she had found first and who had agreed, after some protracted haggling over the fee she would pay for his help, to make the journey to Toulon. As Bruno had suggested to Rosa, it was unlikely she would find anyone to take them directly to Marseilles.

Brian had seemed very business-like. The trip would be better made at night, he said – safer, more plausible – and he would ensure by nightfall that he had some suitable fish on board to suggest a genuine fishing trip. When his passengers had boarded in the twilight, the first thing he had done was to show them where to hide if a patrol boat were to approach and insist on a search. 'Unlikely,' he had said, 'but not impossible. What they call the "Phoney War" in the Med is coming to an end. Everyone's jumpy. The French, the Italians, the British. It's all going to change soon and this whole place will become hell.'

Their hiding place, should it be needed, was a void beneath the deck, the housing for the steering shaft. Having instructed his passengers, Brian cast off, pulling quietly out of the harbour. To the east of the town, the great Genoese citadel squatted roundly and immovably, its Argos eyes dimming as night fell.

Later in the evening, with Carlo eventually asleep, Rosa joined Brian in the small wheel room. She told him how grateful she was for his help.

'Well, you're paying me well, so it's hardly a favour... Actually, I love coming out at night. I love the Mediterranean at night. It's womb-like... the enclosed waters of the womb. And when you think of the civilisations it has given birth to – Islam, Egypt, Rome, Italy, Venice, Greece. Staggering, really.'

She nodded. There was silence for a moment and then she asked, 'So what's a Frenchman doing calling himself Brian?' She felt instinctively safe with the man, unlike with Pietro, and did not feel that she was being over-familiar.

'Blame my mother!' he replied. 'She's Irish and insisted on Brian. My father wasn't very pleased! He wanted to call me Loïc.'

'Was he a fisherman?'

'He was. And always very amused to be a Boucher! The butcher fisherman! ...And you?' he asked. 'What brings you on this perilous journey? Are you running from something?'

'Sort of,' she said. 'I'm taking this little boy to people who can look after him. I am... I was his nanny.'

'Nanny. Ah! And where are his parents?'

'They're dead, Brian ...That's why I'm taking this strange route to England... to France, then England. I know a family who will look after him.'

He asked her if she had always been a nanny.

'When I was about thirteen, I decided that I wanted to work with children, either as a nanny or a teacher, and eventually I decided it was a nanny I wanted to be. And I also wanted some adventure. So I went to England to train at a prestigious school in Kent, grandly titled "The Training School for Ladies' Nurses".' She chuckled as she said the name.

'And did you enjoy England?'

'I did. I liked the people. And the other students. One I became great friends with. Peggy. We had lots of fun together. And got in few scrapes! ...And once she invited me for a long weekend to her aunt's in the West Country. A lovely woman, Dora, a farmer's wife. And Dora said that if I was ever in the country again, I should visit and spend longer with them. I just know that she will welcome us and will make sure that little Carlo will be safe... So. That's where I'm hoping to get to now.'

'You've got a long way still to go, haven't you? Do you think you'll make it?'

'I do. I think I'm a lucky person. Always had luck on my side. When I was at the training college, just about to finish, the principal called me in one day – a strict, starchy old woman, but helpful and very fair – and she said that I was to be interviewed for the position as nanny to one of the grandchildren of Victor Emmanuel III, the King of Italy.'

'Royalty! My word!' said Brian, doing an exaggeratedly fawning bow. 'I have a Very Important Person on board!'

'Says the son of a republican Irish mother and a republican French father!'

They both laughed.

'I enjoyed my time there and settled in quickly. It was fascinating. And I quickly had to learn the idiosyncrasies of relationships within the household. And I realised that the convolutions of the various and extensive branches of the House of Savoy required very careful navigation!'

'They're all mad, aren't they, the royal families of Europe? Inbred and mad!'

'I don't know about that. Princess Marie was lovely. I adored her and did a very good job, I know. And got on well with the mother.'

'So is this little chap' – he pointed towards the cabin – 'one of the family?'

Rosa shook her head. 'No. The thing is I didn't have long with Princess Marie. The war was approaching and Germany – Hitler – was trying to forge closer ties with Italy. At just the wrong time someone discovered that I was half-Jewish and was therefore no longer a desirable presence in the household. So I was given my marching orders. I headed north and was lucky to—'

'Hang on...' Brian picked up a pair of binoculars and scanned ahead. 'I think we may have company heading our way.'

Rosa went into the cabin and gently woke up Carlo. 'Carlo, my darling boy, we need to hide for a while under the deck. Do you remember the man telling us that we might have to?'

Carlo sat up, nodded blearily, let out a complaining moan and slid from the bench. When the vessel was not more than five hundred yards away, Brian pulled at the metal ring on the deck panel to lift it up. Carlo got into the pit, fitting comfortably one side of the steering shaft, while Rosa lowered herself awkwardly the other side. The utter blackness, the loud rumbling noise of the water underneath the boat, the stench of oil, all combined into an aggressive assault on the senses. Rosa was unsure how long either she or Carlo could remain in this increasingly airless prison. She heard the boat approaching. Was it slowing? Yes... No; it seemed not, after all. And soon the sound receded and the hatch was opened by Brian.

13th April 1940

'Is that the one we're going on?' Carlo asked. He was pointing into the sky at an aeroplane that was coming in to land at the airport outside Marseilles.

'No, my darling,' Rosa replied. 'We're going to go on a flying boat from the lake.'

They could see Lake Marignane from the lodgings that Rosa had secured for the night.

'From the lake!' Carlo exploded into a laugh, the first time he had laughed or even smiled since leaving Trieste. 'Do aeroplanes float?' he asked with an amused grin on his face.

'Flying boats do.'

'Flying *boats*!' he cried. Rosa wanted to hug him for joy as he cackled with delight. 'I've never, never ever seen a boat that could fly!'

'Well, they're specially made, darling. The bottom of the fuselage... Fuselage?' He shook his head. 'The bottom of the main part of the plane is shaped like a boat. And the wings have floats fixed to them.'

'And we're going to go on one?'

'We are, my darling. When I can arrange it.'

After a train journey from Toulon to Marseilles and then an ancient, rattly bus to the airport, Rosa had discovered that the person she needed to talk to was the Station Operations Officer for the British Airways Overseas Corporation. She had asked for the Imperial Airways Line office – that was the name in her planned itinerary – but it had very recently been taken over by the new organisation, she was told.

The man she had dealt with was called Jimmy. He was nice enough but had just laughed when she said he had no ticket.

This was the moment for her to produce what she had always regarded as the talismans that would enable her to reach safety. She dug into her Gladstone bag and pulled out a wooden plaque – a red shield with a white cross held by two lions, with a crowned golden eagle above, all framed in a red, ermine-lined robe with gold trimmings: the coat of arms of the House of Savoy. She also withdrew from an envelope a letter and a signet ring. Both carried the same coat of arms.

'Jimmy – may I call you that?' She was sure that she would be able to. From the start, she had seen in Jimmy's eyes a look of interest that she knew signified attraction and which she was sure that she could transmute very easily into lust. 'Jimmy,' she said, 'can we talk where we will not be overheard?'

Once outside the prefabricated office hut she showed him her talisman. 'Jimmy, this is a difficult matter... The boy in my care is a prince. He is the grandchild of Victor Emmanuel, the King of Italy. The monarchy is about to be toppled and I have been asked to deliver the boy, Prince Carlo, safely to England. For his safety.'

Jimmy was looking surprised, then interested, then conspiratorial. 'Gosh... yes... of course... But surely there are official papers and things. I mean... I presume it has been passed through the appropriate channels.'

'We had no time, I'm afraid, Jimmy. We had to flee Rome very quickly. That's why I haven't even got Carlo's – Prince Carlo's – passport and papers... The journey we've had! You wouldn't believe it!'

'And who exactly are you? I mean, I'm sorry, that sounded rude... I just need to get things straight in my head.'

'I am the nanny of Prince Carlo's sister, Princess Marie. And more generally, a guardian of all the children.'

Rosa passed Jimmy the letter of appointment: thick, expensive paper with a colourful embossed crest of the House of Savoy. The letter was genuinely hers. The plaque with the coat of arms and the signet ring, together with a considerable sum of money, she had stolen from the family when she had been summarily dismissed for her part-Jewish ancestry. She pointed to the relevant paragraph of the letter which, in addition to detailing her duties as 'Children's Nurse' to Princess Marie, gave her the more general duty of 'attending to the needs of the other children of the household as required'.

'Madam, I will need to get some kind of clearance for this.'

'Rosa. Call me Rosa, Jimmy.' She moved closer, not quite touching him, but close enough for him to feel her breath on his face. 'Jimmy, for reasons which are really quite complicated, this has to be done on the quiet. Believe me, once we're safely in England, you will be commended for your quick initiative.'

Jimmy was looking her in the eye. In his own eyes she could see a battle raging between duty and desire.

'Look, Jimmy, I've got to find lodgings tonight for the two of us, but once I've got that fixed, perhaps we could meet up for a drink and discuss this more fully.'

As she took her letter of appointment back from him, she allowed her hand to linger a little over his.

He nodded.

*

When Rosa returned to the lodgings later that evening the landlady reassured her that Carlo had not woken. He opened his eyes briefly as Rosa climbed into the bed alongside him and fell quickly back into sleep again. She had allowed Jimmy the intimacies he had sought with her and she had extracted a promise – how reliable, she was unsure – that he would place her and 'the prince' on a plane bound for Poole, in England, in two days' time. It would be stopping on its way from Rangoon. Two passengers would be terminating their journey at Marseilles, and their places, Jimmy promised, would be allocated to Rosa.

She slept fitfully. Carlo was restless, turning frequently, emitting stifled groans, his tired body twitching. In the early morning she was awoken by a terrified scream that morphed into a hoarse wail. She brought the boy gently out of his nightmare, clasping him to her, stroking his head and soothing him with quiet, gentle words. 'It's all right, Carlo, it's all right, my darling.'

He fell asleep quickly once more, clutching his shoes, which he habitually took to bed with him, leaving Rosa to relive the contents of his dream.

On their final morning in Trieste, she and Carlo had left the apartment of Bosco and Maria for a mid-morning walk into the centre of town. Carlo wanted to pop into his father's shop. He loved the smell of leather that filled every nook and cranny of it. When fresh stock arrived, he had to check and feel and smell and admire each new line.

He had cuddled his mother before leaving with Rosa and had kissed his older brother on the cheek. Alfonso was not at school, as normal. He had complained to his mother of a severe headache and disturbed vision, so she had kept him at home for the day.

As the nanny and boy were about to turn the final street corner towards Bosco's shop, they could hear a commotion. Loud, ugly voices and the crackling of shattering glass. People were milling around, some hurrying away, some trying to position themselves for a better view of what was going on.

When Rosa saw what it was, she put a hand across Carlo's eyes and tried to wheel him quickly away. But he escaped her clutch and ran towards the scene, screaming, 'Papa! Papa!'

Bosco was on the ground now, on his hands and his knees, with blood pouring from a head wound. Three balaclava-ed men with clubs stood around him, one of them bringing his weapon so brutally down upon Bosco's back that his hands shot out in front of him and his head banged heavily onto the pavement with a crack.

She was sure that one of these three men had caught sight of her as she had quickly reached to gather Carlo when he moved towards his father, snatching him roughly and leading him away at a run in the opposite direction. She had wanted to run home, to the safety of the apartment but, while she was still within earshot of the Black Shirts who were killing Bosco, she had heard one shout to two of his ransacking colleagues, 'Get up to the Goretti place. Whoever's there, take care of them.'

14th April 1940

There was little to do but wait to see whether Jimmy would be as good as his word and the following day get them aboard the plane bound for England. The landlady suggested that Rosa take Carlo out to look at the aeroplanes to keep him occupied. He couldn't understand the two women, who were talking French, but, when the landlady smiled towards him and gestured with her arms the motion of flying, he understood immediately and nodded a smiling face.

'The planes, Rosa! Are we going to see the planes?' he asked excitedly. 'Yes, yes! And the flying boats?'

With a simple picnic prepared by the landlady they set off for the Etang de Bolmon. There was a cool April breeze blowing in, so Rosa had to wrap Carlo in one of her cardigans. Not that he needed it; he was too excited to notice the cold.

They found a sheltered spot out of the breeze. It had the additional advantage of a large fallen tree on which they could sit to eat and from which they could watch the unfolding display. To the east Carlo could see planes coming and going from the landing strip, and to the north an occasional flying boat would land or take off on the lake.

Some of the flying boats were small and landed like over-large insects skidding across the water. During the afternoon a large plane came in. Its stout fuselage had a curved underbelly that rose into a stubby snout at the front. The wings were mounted high in the main body, each with two propeller engines and each with a pontoon suspended below for buoyancy on the water.

Carlo was thrilled. 'I hope that's the one we're going on, Rosa!'

'We'll see, darling, we'll see… I hope so!'

She loved his excitement. It was what she had become used to in Trieste: an optimistic little boy with an unquenchable enthusiasm for anything new; with a curiosity, she felt sure, that would develop as he grew up and went to school – to university, perhaps – into a formidable intelligence.

She wondered how damaged that delicate mechanism of mind had been by the events he had witnessed in Trieste. She had dared not talk about the incident or about his parents, preferring to point his attention towards the future, towards what she hoped would be the safe haven of Dora Abbott's farm in Devon.

'You are my little prince,' she said to him. 'Prince Carlo. Son of Umberto and Maria. And you are going to start a new life with some wonderful people in a lovely new country. I know you will be happy, darling.'

'You'll be there to look after me, won't you, Rosa?'

'Of course… Of course.' Did Carlo notice the sadness in her voice as she repeated the phrase? She hoped not.

One thing she knew for sure was that she would not be allowed to stay with him. She would be entering the country illegally and would either be summarily deported or sent to an internment camp somewhere in England.

For the moment, all she could do was smother him with love, fill him with a sense of security and ensure that he reached the intended destination safely. If she did these things successfully, she would feel satisfied and happy. In any case, his love, his affection, the cheerfulness that he found somewhere in that traumatised mind of his were more than enough reward for her.

15th April 1940

Rosa and Carlo were sitting in the aft cabin, facing into the aisle. The aisle of a Short S.23 Empire C-Class Flying Boat, Carlo had been informed by the clerk who checked the passenger list. Before the excitement of coming aboard, they had been weighed so that the distribution in the plane, which also carried a heavy payload of Air Mail, could be calculated. 'Half a stone of nothing,' the officer had said as he placed the little boy on the scales. 'I don't think we'll need to put a stamp on you, young man!'

Carlo was disappointed that he was not by a window and that he would have to remain in his seat for the take-off and landing. But when the engines came to life with a great roar he could barely contain his excitement. There was a moment of agitation when every part of the aircraft broke into a noisy vibration, but he was soon grinning again as it began to move, the sound of the water slapping and slushing against the hull beneath their feet. As the plane turned into the wind for take-off, there was a high-pitched whine and rumble, and then a booming roar of propellers and a deepening engine note as the hull broke free from the foaming water and lifted into the air.

Rosa did not enjoy the experience. She had only flown twice before and had hated it on both occasions. As the motors continued to whine and the metal wings and fuselage grumbled and groaned, she felt fearful. But it made her happy, and it distracted her, to her see the look of complete exhilaration, of release, on Carlo's young face.

The cabin wasn't pressurised so they could not climb beyond 10,000 feet, but nevertheless it was cold and soon the two of them were sharing a blanket and wearing the footmuffs that had been provided for passengers, much to Carlo's amused delight. Soon enough, the excitement done for the time being, he fell into a peaceful sleep.

The landing in England, on the placid waters of Poole Harbour, was smooth. After a delay while the plane was moored to buoys, the doors were opened to reveal a launch waiting to take them to the wooden jetty and the makeshift, unfinished BOAC terminal.

Here they would be processed. And, Rosa fervently hoped, cleared for further progress.

The officer who checked Rosa's papers read them with careful concentration, looking puzzled at first and then nodding his head, staring with interest at Carlo before speaking to Rosa. He read out the address that Jimmy's notes contained, the address of Dora Abbott in Devon, asking her to confirm that this was her destination, and then explaining to her what she must do.

'You will need, when you arrive, madam, to report to the local police station. I shall be wiring them to expect you in the next day or two.' Rosa nodded. She knew that her alien status required notification to the authorities.

They spent the night in a hotel that overlooked the harbour mouth and in the morning were given a lift to the station. With a warming spring sun in the sky reflecting pretty, silvery patterns on the extensive waters of the harbour, Rosa felt sure that the signs for Carlo's beginnings in England were propitious.

20

It seemed an age ago that I started the story of Carlo d'Abruzzi by writing the opening chapter of a biography that had him arriving in Liverpool, a stylishly dressed and ambitiously determined young man striding towards the record shop of Brian Epstein with news of the Beatles. Poor Carlo. Confused at the end, frightened by the lies his loving daughter had believed and wanted told to the world. He could hardly remember some of the details of the backstory he had invented for himself. It was a frightened, confused man who had wandered absent-mindedly in front of a bus in Hammersmith Broadway. With his death a new life would emerge, the real story of the man, less exotic than the story that Theresa had believed since childhood, but no less interesting and, in its own way, no less heroic.

When I finished writing the new opening chapter to his life – the life of Carlo Goretti, son of a shop owner in Trieste – I decided that it was time to tie up loose ends. I wanted to hand over to Luca and Theresa the fruits of all my researches and close the book, so to speak, on the d'Abruzzi and Goretti families. Ideally I wanted a formal conclusion to the business – a dinner somewhere, if Luca would allow it, with me, with the d'Abruzzi twins, and with Angelo and Helen Goretti. And I wanted – a sticking point with Luca, possibly – George Nelson to be there at the beginning to photograph the gathered group. George it was, after all – roguish George – who had crashed Carlo's funeral and enabled, through his prying photographs, Angelo to emerge and Angelo to be located; he it was, too, who had discovered the address of the farm where Carlo had grown up. The farm, I knew, would be a necessary place of pilgrimage for Theresa, so I also wanted to check with Rosie Barlow that she was as good as her word and would welcome the twins to Highfold Farm.

I had recently learnt, since finishing my narrative version of Rosa's journal, of another piece of the jigsaw of Carlo's life. And wouldn't it have to have been George who came up with it! Convalescing from his misfortune on the back of his accomplice's motorbike, he had found himself unable to work, either as a pap, which required rather more dexterity and agility than he currently had, or as a photojournalist, which career was still in an embryonic state, so he had decided to do some research into Carlo himself. 'Just out of curiosity, mate,' he would tell me.

I was summoned for a pub lunch and hailed noisily with the customary 'Nickolai!', as I walked to the bar.

'Not working, George?'

'Not at the moment, mate. Still got a lotta pain. Leg. Ribs. Arm. Bonce!' He tapped his head. 'It's done me 'ead in, I gotta tell ya. I'm done with the pap lark and to be honest, Nick, I think I want to get out of London. Sell up. Go back to Reading. Set up a posh studio. Portraits. Weddings. Uni graduations. That kind of malarkey. The quiet life.'

I was surprised. I couldn't imagine him enjoying the quiet life for more than a few days. He must have seen my scepticism. His face broke into teasing grin. 'Either that, mate, or... or, Nichol-arse, son, I might become a private eye! You've got me interested!'

'*I've* got you interested? Come off it, George!'

'No, honest injun, mate. Photographing that car and tracing that Angel Gretto feller for you... finding that farm in, where was it? The West Country. Made me fink. And I've made another little discovery while you've been busy.'

'Okay...?' I said, wondering what on earth he'd been up to now.

'That ol' mucker what died... Charlo... Charlo Debruisee.' He paused until he was happy that my interest was fully enough piqued and was registering satisfactorily on my face. 'Well, mate, me ol' mucker... He had a spell on Funny Farm—'

'Funny Farm?'

'Doolally, mate. Round the twist... Two bales short of—'

'I know what Funny Farm is, George, thank you. I'm just surprised.'

But actually I wasn't when I thought about it. According to George, he'd been sectioned in 1965 and spent a while in an institution in North London, becoming a postman only once he was deemed fit to go out into society again. Molly, the librarian in Brixton, had mentioned Carlo's witnessing of a vicious attack when he had been doing a milk round. I wondered if it was this that had triggered the final breakdown.

Small wonder that the mind of the young man had been beset with so much disturbance. As far as I could see, he had never had the chance to work through the trauma of seeing his father murdered, seeing his mother and brother for the last time on that same day, and losing, within a fortnight, Rosa, the last fixed point of his life at that time. Poor Carlo, carrying that terrible darkness within him, like some slowly developing parasite, burrowing and growing inwardly during his childhood years and into his young adulthood. Until it resurfaced.

*

We met in a restaurant in West London. Luca had written a most gracious letter to me after I had got in touch with him. I'd emailed him my new opening chapter of his father's life, together with the details of Angelo and Helen Goretti, and of Rosie Barlow and Highfold Farm; and I had posted him Rosa's journal and the translation of it. I made him aware that Rosie would be delighted to have him and his sister to stay any time they wanted and that she had a box containing some of Carlo's childhood things which they would find fascinating.

Luca came back to me a few days later to say that Theresa was in an improved state of mind and that she had been very moved by everything I'd sent and everything I'd done. She would be happy for us all to gather together and was excited about meeting her cousin. It had pleased her to hear that the Gorettis would be staying in London for a couple of nights so that there would be opportunities to get to know their new-found relatives better.

I was the first to arrive at the restaurant, followed shortly by Luca, who had, predictably, vetoed the presence of George and camera. He was uncharacteristically warm; grateful, he told me, for all that I had done, unbidden though it was. The Gorettis were the next to arrive, Helen's face a picture as she saw in Luca the younger incarnation of her husband.

And then Theresa. Was she apprehensive about the meeting, this young woman who had seemed so completely confident when I had first met her in what seemed another lifetime? Probably. She gave me a smile and, while I wouldn't say it was false, there was a certain stiffness to it. And then she caught sight of Angelo. A flicker of astonishment, followed by a sunburst of complete delight.

'My cousin!' she cried, rushing to hug him. 'My long-lost cousin!' There were tears and the inarticulate sounds of emotions beyond words. Even Luca, with his lawyer's coolness, seemed moved.

When we sat down I had a feeling that I didn't really belong at this gathering. But then Helen, who perhaps felt something of an outsider too, said, 'How incredible that Nick was able to uncover all this history for us!', drawing all eyes towards me.

'Yes, indeed. Incredible. And wonderful.' It was Angelo who spoke. Luca nodded, his face impassive, and Theresa looked towards me. The expression was deep, not the smile she had given me when she had entered the restaurant, but a look of complex and perhaps contrary emotions that she perhaps couldn't fully process, still less could I.

'Yes, Nick, you've done a great job, and we're very grateful.'

We ordered drinks and looked at the menu, a glance at which, with its inventive dishes and exorbitant prices, suggested that Luca's insistence that he pay for us all was no light undertaking. Food apart, it was not an ideal place to meet. The fashionably bare brick walls, flag-stone floor and solid, uncushioned furniture created a harsh ambience, a sharpness of sound where the occasion seemed to demand something softer.

'I gather you have arranged to go and stay with the Barlows in Devon,' I said to Theresa.

'Yes. I'm going the weekend after next. I asked Luca to come with me, but he's busy and says he will go another time, perhaps… Rosie sounded very nice.'

'She is. Absolutely lovely. You'll get on very well, and she will love showing you the house and the farm.' I didn't like to mention Carlo's childhood treasure chest, which I knew Rosie would show her and which equally I knew would create an emotional storm-burst in Theresa.

Both the twins wanted to hear a full account of Angelo's story, so once again he had to negotiate the minefield of feelings about the day his grandfather, Bosco, was murdered. He had struggled in telling me when I had visited him in Watford, and naturally found it difficult to tell the story again to his new listeners, going haltingly once more through the chilling details. As he told of his father's escape, the sound of his voice seemed to rebound off the unplastered, unadorned walls.

'One of the staff who had hurried from the shop was screaming at my grandmother and father to pack a bag as quickly as they could and run for it. Bosco had been clubbed to death outside the shop, he told them, and the fascist thugs were coming for them now. They must flee immediately, not a second to be lost… So they hastily gathered some things

– some food, some clothes, some money – and they fled. But not before my grandmother had written an address on a slip of paper to give the man from the shop. "This is where we are going, if we can get there. Please try to get this address to Rosa and ask her to bring Carlo to me." And then they went. Got a bus out of town and then a train to Ljubljana, where there was a second cousin who Bosco had kept in touch with.'

There was another pause. Another struggle to maintain control of his voice. 'And they never saw Carlo again.' Drawing an audible gasp and cry from Theresa, whose tears had been steadily welling. 'After the war, they returned to Trieste to look for him and Rosa. But nothing. They were told – they never knew how reliably – that Rosa had fled with Carlo to England. But they never heard from him or Rosa and assumed that they had been killed on the journey... My grandmother died in 1949 – my father always believed it was of a broken heart. He was nineteen, the same age as Bosco when his father died.'

Theresa was now sobbing, which had released tears in Angelo. Luca took his sister's hand and Helen rose to stand behind Theresa and Angelo, a comforting hand on each shoulder.

Later in the meal Luca, in his characteristically dry tone, asked about Rosa. 'Rosa is something of a heroine in this story – certainly that's the impression you get from her journal, and from the account you wrote up, Nick. Do we know what became of her?'

'I did try to find out, Luca. There are various lists of aliens in the Second World War, which you can check online. Many of the aliens – terrible word – were sent to internment camps.

That is what would have happened to Rosa. If you remember, when she arrived in Poole, she was told to report to the local police station in Devon when she got to the farm. I'm not sure she ever did that. I think she probably stayed a few days with the Abbotts, making sure that Carlo settled in, and then just disappeared. Where? We just don't know. She may have assumed a false identity. May have tried to get back to Italy, though that would have been difficult with France overrun and Italy now in the war... Pretty much impossible.'

'It would be fascinating to find out,' said Helen.

*

For all the tears, the heightened, raw emotions, it was a happy lunch. And centre-stage, as he should have been, was Carlo, very much present in the reanimations of Theresa and Angelo.

Angelo recalled some of his father, Alfonso's, memories of Carlo. 'Carlo was five years younger, and I think Dad always felt very protective. He said that Carlo was a very sensitive child, easily frightened and easily hurt if someone said something unkind. But very generous, always, he said. And very gentle... He had a vivid memory of Carlo one day finding a wounded bird on the balcony of their apartment – Dad couldn't remember whether it was a corvid of some kind, or blackbird, or a dove, even. But when Carlo found it he asked his mother for a box and some scraps of torn paper and something to put some water in. And he put the bird in the box with some water and some bits of bread and nursed it for a few days, leaving it out on the balcony at night, till one morning it was gone.'

'Ah, that's such a sweet story, Angelo.' Theresa's own childhood memories were swirling through her head and she lighted upon a sailing trip that she and Luca had been taken on by their parents. A friend of the family had a yacht moored on the River Frome near Wareham and had invited the d'Abruzzis out for a day's sailing in Poole Harbour and the sea beyond. 'It's poignant,' she said, 'to think that he was sailing around the place where he had first made land-fall in England. Do you remember that trip, Luca?'

He nodded. 'I do. Not that we knew that Poole had any special significance for him. He never talked about his escape from Trieste… the incredible journey he made with Rosa.'

'I've got such a vivid memory of that day, Luca. Mum prepared a picnic, which we took to the yacht – smoked salmon sandwiches, some salami, strawberries and some fizzy drinks. Glorious sunny day. Perfect. And we headed down the river into the harbour. And we stopped at Brownsea Island and saw some red squirrels, didn't we?'

'We did! It's all beginning to come back to me now!' There was an excitement in Luca's voice that I had never heard before.

'And then we sailed out of the harbour mouth past the chain ferry into the open sea. Gosh, I remember the swell in that narrow mouth. The yacht heaving dangerously. Well – I thought it was dangerously! I was scared out of my wits for a moment! How old were we? We must have been seven or eight. Papa saw I was scared and laughed and laughed and sang "Life on the Ocean Wave"! …And do you remember, when a huge ferry came past he pretended to be a Greenpeace eco-warrior, shouting, "Save the whales!" Daft as a brush!'

We were all laughing now at these happy anecdotes about Carlo.

'And we went round the headland and moored in Studland Bay for the picnic, I think, didn't we?'

Theresa nodded. 'And then we went to see Old Harry, those great rock stacks. And Papa said something like, "Of course, I remember him when he was Young Harry, a very, very long time ago. And he was quite something in his prime!"'

More laughter. But suddenly Luca was looking serious, his cheerful mood punctured, the jollity tempered. 'It's very strange, this... but this memory, this sharp memory has come back to me. Completely vivid. It's weird... I last thought about it when I was an English student and was reading TS Eliot's *Four Quartets* and I came across the lines "To make an end is to make a beginning. The end is where we start from". They were oddly familiar to me at the time and I had this powerful sense of déjà vu. I could hear them being said in Dad's voice. But just thought nothing more about them. But they have just flooded back into my head with complete clarity. To make an end is to make a beginning. The end is where we start from. It's what Dad was saying as we came into the harbour on that trip. Mysterious words which we made nothing of as young children... But of course he must have been thinking, as he said those lines, that he was in exactly the place – that part of the harbour – where it started, his life in England, his new life... Remarkable.'

Remarkable indeed. And Carlo d'Abruzzi was indeed a remarkable man. Sadly, however, the book I had started to write about him – twice started to write – was a book that I would never complete.

*

It was time to say our goodbyes. We embraced as we uttered our farewells, the Gorettis first, and then Luca. And finally Theresa. Beautiful Theresa. That lovely face, those enchanting dancing eyes that I had half fallen in love with. And as I embraced her, the familiar fragrance, the mingled aromas of her body and her perfume, filled me once more with longing.

'You're a star, Theresa,' I said. 'I'm sure everything will work out just fine.'

'Thank you, Nick. And thank you for all you've done. You've been very good.'

The beginnings of an autumn chill were in the air. As we uttered our prosaic farewells, we both knew that our briefly intersecting lives were heading in directions that would never again cross; and that there would be no shadow of another parting.